THREE HEARTS AND
THREE LIONS

Books by Poul Anderson

Novels

Agent of the Terran Empire
The Avatar
The Boat of a Million Years
Brain Wave
The Broken Sword
The Byworlder
A Circus of Hells
Cold Victory
Conan the Rebel
The Corridors of Time
The Dancer From Atlantis
The Day of Their Return
The Devil's Game
The Earth Book of Stormgate
Ensign Flandry
Fire Time
Flandry of Terra
The Fleet of Stars
For Love and Glory
The Game of Empire
Genesis
Harvest of Stars
Harvest the Fire
The High Crusade
Hrolf Kraki's Saga
A Knight of Ghosts and Shadows
The Long Night
Maurai and Kith
The Merman's Children
A Midsummer Tempest
Mirkheim
Mother of Kings
New America
No World of Their Own
Operation Chaos
Operation Luna
Orbit Unlimited
Orion Shall Rise
The People of the Wind
Planet of No Return
The Psychotechnic League
The Rebel Worlds

Shield
The Shield of Time
Starfarers
Starship
The Stars Are Also Fire
A Stone in Heaven
Tau Zero
There Will Be Time
Three Worlds to Conquer
The Time Patrol
Trader to the Stars
The Trouble Twisters
Twilight World
Vault of the Ages
War of the Gods
War of the Wing-Men
War of Two Worlds
The Winter of the World
World Without Stars

Hokas
(with Gordon R. Dickson)
Hoka! Hoka! Hoka!
Hokas Pokas

The King of Ys
(with Karen Anderson)
Roma Mater
Gallicenae
Dahut
The Dog and the Wolf

Short Fiction
Alight in the Void
All One Universe
The Best of Poul Anderson
The Dark Between the Stars
The Enemy Stars
Going for Infinity
Kinship with the Stars
The Many Worlds of Poul Anderson
Tales of the Flying Mountains
Time and Stars

SFBC 50TH
ANNIVERSARY COLLECTION

Three Hearts and Three Lions

Poul Anderson

50 YEARS SFBC FANTASY
4

To

Robert and Karen Hertz

NOTE

AFTER SO MUCH time has passed, I feel obliged to write this down. Holger and I first met more than twenty years ago. It was in another generation—another age. The bright lads whom I am training these days are friendly and all that, but we don't think the same language and there's no use pretending otherwise. I have no idea whether they will be able to accept a yarn like this. They are a more sober lot than my friends and I were; they seem to get less fun out of life. On the other hand, they have grown up with the incredible. Look at any scientific journal, any newspaper, out of any window, and ask yourself if outlandishness has not become the ordinary way of the world.

Holger's tale does not seem altogether impossible to me. Not that I claim it's true. I have no proof one way or the other. My hope is just that it shall not quite be lost. Assume, for argument's sake, that what I heard was fact. Then there are implications for our own future, and we'll have use for the knowledge Assume, what is of course far sensible, that I record only a dream, or a very tall story. Then I still think it's worth preserving for its own sake.

This much is certainly true: Holger Carlsen came to work for the engineering outfit that employed me, in the fall of that remote year 1938. During the months which followed, I got to know him quite well.

He was a Dane, and like most young Scandinavians had a powerful hankering to see the world. As a boy, he had traveled by foot or bicycle across most of Europe. Later, full of his countrymen's traditional admiration for the United States, he wangled a scholarship to one of our Eastern universities, where he studied mechanical engineering. His summers he spent hitchhiking and odd-jobbing around North America. He liked the land so much that after he graduated he obtained a position here and thought seriously of getting naturalized.

We were all his friends. He was an amiable, slow-spoken fellow, thoroughly down to earth, with simple tastes in living style and humor—though every so often he broke loose and went to a certain Danish restaurant to gorge on *smorrebrod* and *akvavit*. As an engineer he was satisfactory if unspectacular, his talents running more toward rule-of-thumb practicality than the analytical approach. In short, he was in no way remarkable mentally.

His physique was a different matter. He was gigantic, six feet four and so broad in the shoulders that he didn't look his height. He'd played football, of course, and could have starred on his college team if his studies hadn't taken too much time. His face was of the rugged sort, square, with high cheekbones, cleft chin, a slightly dented nose, yellow hair and wide-set blue eyes. Given better technique, by which I mean less worry about hurting their feelings, he could have cut a swathe through the local femininity. But as it was, that slight shyness probably kept him from more than his share of such adventures. All in all, Holger was a nice average guy, what was later called a good Joe.

He told me something about his background. "Believe it or not," he grinned, "I really vas the baby in the cartoons, you know, the vun left on the doorstep. I must have been only a few days old ven I vas found in a courtyard in Helsnigor. That's the very pretty place you call Elsinore, Hamlet's home town. I never learned vere I came from. Such happenings is very rare in Denmark, and the police tried hard to find out, but they never did. I vas soon adopted by the Carlsen family. Otherwise there is not'ing unusual in my life."

That's what he thought.

I remember one time I persuaded him to go with me to a lecture by a visiting physicist: one of those magnificent types which only Britain seems to produce, scientist, philosopher, poet, social critic, wit, the Renaissance come back in a gentler shape. This man was discussing the new cosmology. Since then the physicists have gone further, but even in those days educated people used to hark back with a certain wistfulness to times when the universe was merely strange—not incomprehensible. He wound up his talk with some frank speculation about what we might discover in the future. If relativity and quantum mechanics have proven that the observer is inseparable from the world he observes, if logical positivism has demonstrated how many of our supposedly solid facts are mere constructs and conventions, if the psychic researchers have shown man's mind to possess unsuspected powers, it begins to look as if some of those old myths and sorceries were a bit more than superstition. Hypnotism and the curing of psychosomatic conditions by faith were once dismissed as legend. How much of what we dismiss today may have been based on fragmentary observation, centuries ago, before the very existence of a scientific framework began to condition what facts we would and would not discover? And this is only a question about our own world. What of other universes? Wave mechanics already admits the possibility of one entire cosmos coexisting with ours. The lecturer said it was not hard to write the equations for an infinity of such parallel worlds. By logical necessity the laws of nature would vary from one to another. Therefore, somewhere in the boundlessness of reality, anything you can imagine must actually exist!

Holger yawned through most of this, and made sarcastic remarks when we were having a drink afterward. "These mat'ematicians vork their brains so hard, no vonder they snap into metaphysics ven off duty. Eqval and opposite reaction."

"You're using the right term," I teased him, "though you don't mean to."

"Vat's that?"

" 'Metaphysics.' The word means, literally, after or beyond physics. In other words, when the physics you know, the kind you measure with your instruments and calculate with your slide rule, when that ends, metaphysics begins. And that's where we are right now, my lad: at the beginning of being beyond physics."

"Voof!" He gulped down his drink and gestured for another. "It has rubbed off on you."

"Well, maybe. But think a minute. Do we really *know* the dimensions of physics? Don't we define them purely with respect to each other? In an absolute sense, Holger, what are you? Where are you? Or, rather, what-where-when are you?"

"I'm me, here and now, drinking some not very good liquor."

"You're in balance—in tune with?—in the matrix of?—a specific continuum. So am I; the same for both of us. That continuum embodies a specific set of mathematical relationships among such dimensions as space, time, and energy. We know some of those relationships, under the name 'natural laws.' Hence we have organized bodies of knowledge we call physics, astronomy, chemistry——"

"And voodoo!" He lifted his glass. "Time you stopped t'inking and begun some serious drinking. *Skaal!*"

I let it go. Holger didn't mention the subject again. But he must have remembered what was said. Perhaps it even helped him a bit, long afterward. I dare hope so.

The war broke out overseas, and Holger started to fret. As the months passed, he grew steadily more unhappy. He had no deep political convictions, but he found he hated the Nazis with a fervor that astonished us both. When the Germans entered his country, he went on a three-day jag.

However, the occupation began fairly peacefully. The Danish government had swallowed the bitter pill, remained at home—the only such government which did—and accepted the status of a neutral power under German protection. Don't think that didn't take courage. Among other things, it meant the king was for some years able to prevent the outrages, especially upon Jews, which the citizens of other occupied nations suffered.

Holger cheered, though, when Denmark's ambassador to the United States declared for the Allies and authorized our entry into Greenland. About this time, most of us realized that America would sooner or later be drawn into the war. The obvious plan for Holger was to await that day, then join the Army. Or he could sign up now with the British or the Free Norwegians. He admitted to me, often, hurt and puzzled at himself, that he couldn't understand what was preventing him.

But by 1941 the news was that Denmark had had enough. Not yet had matters developed to the explosion which finally came, when a national strike led to the Germans ousting the royal government and ruling the country as another conquered province. But already you were beginning to hear gunshots and dynamite. It took Holger a lot of time and beer to make up his mind. Somehow he had gotten a fixation that he must return home.

That didn't make sense, but he couldn't get rid of it, and finally he yielded. At seventh and last, as his people say, he was not an American but a Dane. He quit his job, we gave him a farewell party, and he sailed off on a Swedish ship. From Hälsingborg he could take a ferry home.

I imagine the Germans kept an eye on him for a while. He gave them no trouble, but worked quietly at Burmeister & Wain, the marine engine manufacturers. In mid-1942, when he judged the Nazis had lost interest in him, he joined the underground . . . and was in a uniquely good position for sabotage.

The story of his labors doesn't concern us here. He must have done well. The whole organization did; they were so efficient, and in such close liaison with the British, that few air raids ever needed to be carried out on their territory. In the latter part of 1943 they brought off their greatest exploit.

There was a man who had to be gotten out of Denmark. The Allies needed his information and abilities rather badly. The Germans held him under close watch, for they also knew what he was. Nevertheless, the underground spirited him from his home and conveyed him down to the Sound. A boat lay ready to take him to Sweden, whence he could be flown to England.

We will probably never know whether the Gestapo was on his trail or whether a German patrol simply happened to spot men on the shore long after curfew. Someone cried out, someone else fired, and the battle started. The beach was open and stony, with just enough light to see by from the stars and the illuminated Swedish coast. No way of retreat. The boat got going, and the underground band settled down to hold off the enemy till it had reached the opposite shore.

Their hope even of that was not large. The boat was slow. Their very defense had betrayed its importance. In a few minutes, when the Danes were killed, one of the Germans would break into the nearest house and telephone occupation headquarters in Elsinore, which was not far off. A highpowered motorcraft would intercept the fugitive before he reached neutral territory. However, the underground men did their best.

Holger Carlsen fully expected to die, but he lacked time to be afraid. A part of him remembered other days here, sunlit stillness and gulls overhead, his foster parents, a house full of small dear objects; yes, and Kronborg Castle, red brick and slim towers, patinaed copper roofs above bright waters, why should he suddenly think of Kronborg? He crouched on the shingle, the Luger hot in his fingers, and fired at shadowy leaping forms. Bullets whined by his ears. A man screamed. Holger took aim and shot.

Then all his world blew up in flame and darkness.

1

HE WOKE SLOWLY. For a while he lay unaware of more than the pain in his head. Vision came piecemeal, until he saw that the thing before him was the root of a tree. As he turned over, a thick carpet of leaves crackled. Earth and moss and moisture made a pungency in his nose.

"Det var som fanden!" he muttered, which means, roughly, "What the hell!" He sat up.

Touching his head, he felt clotted blood. His mind was still dulled, but he realized that a bullet must have creased his scalp and knocked him out. A few centimeters lower——He shivered.

But what had happened since? He lay in a forest, by daylight. No one else was around. No sign of anyone else. His friends must have escaped, carrying him along, and hidden him in this tract. But why had they removed his clothes and abandoned him?

Stiff, dizzy, mouth dry and evil-tasting, stomach full of hunger, he clutched his head lest it fall into pieces and got up. By the rays slanting between the tree trunks he saw the time was late afternoon. Morning light doesn't have that peculiar golden quality. Heh! He'd almost slept the clock around. He sneezed.

Not far off, a brook tinkled through deep sun-flecked shadows. He went over, stooped, and drank enormously. Afterward he washed his face. The cold water gave him back a little strength. He looked around and tried to think where he might be. Grib's Wood?

No, by Heaven. These trees were too big and gnarly and wild: oak, ash, beech, thorn, densely covered with moss, underbrush tangled between them to form a nearly solid wall. There had been no such area in Denmark since the Middle Ages.

A squirrel ran like a red fire-streak up a bole. A pair of starlings flew away. Through a rift in the leafage he saw a hawk hovering, immensely far above. Were any hawks left in his country?

Well, maybe a few, he didn't know. He looked at his nakedness and wondered groggily what to do next. If he'd been stripped and left here by his comrades there must be a good reason and he shouldn't wander off. Especially in this state of deshabille. On the other hand, something might have happened to them.

"You can hardly camp here overnight, my boy," he said. "Let's at least find out where you are." His voice seemed unnaturally loud where only the forest rustled.

No, another sound. He tensed before recognizing the neigh of a horse. That made him feel better. There must be a farm nearby. His legs were steady enough now that he could push through a screen of withes to find the horse.

When he did, he stopped dead. "No," he said.

The animal was gigantic, a stallion the size of a Percheron but with more graceful build, sleek and black as polished midnight. It was not tethered, though an elaborate fringed pair of reins hung from a headstall chased with silver and arabesques. On its back was a saddle, high in pommel and cantle, also of ornamented leather; a sweeping silken blanket, white with an embroidered black eagle; and a bundle of some kind.

Holger swallowed and approached closer. All right, he thought, so somebody liked to ride around in such style. "Hallo," he called. "Hallo, is anyone there?"

The horse tossed his flowing mane and whinnied as he neared. A soft nose nuzzled his cheek and the big hoofs stamped as if to be off. Holger patted the animal—he'd never seen a horse so friendly to strangers—and looked closer. Engraved in the silver of the headstall was a word in odd, ancient-looking characters: *Papillon.*

"Papillon," he said wonderingly. The horse whinnied again, stamped, and dragged at the bridle he had caught.

"Papillon, is that your name?" Holger stroked him. "French for butterfly, isn't it? Fancy calling a chap your size Butterfly."

The package behind the saddle caught his attention, and he stepped over for a look. What the devil? Chain mail!

"Hallo!" he called again. "Is anyone there? Help!"

A magpie gibed at him.

Staring around, Holger saw a long steel-headed shaft leaned against a tree, with a basket hilt near the end. A lance, before God, a regular medieval lance. Excitement thuttered in him. His restless life had made him less painstakingly law-abiding than most of his countrymen, and he didn't hesitate to untie the bundle and spread it out. He found quite a bit: a byrnie long enough to reach his knees; a conical crimson-plumed helmet, visorless but with a noseguard; a dagger; assorted belts and thongs; the quilted underpadding for armor. Then there were some changes of clothes, consisting of breeches, full-sleeved shirts, tunics, jerkins, cloaks, and so on. Where the cloth was not coarse, gaily dyed linen, it was silk trimmed with fur. Going around to the left side of the horse, he wasn't surprised to find a sword and shield hung on the breeching. The shield was of conventional heraldic form, about four feet long, and obviously new. When he took the canvas cover off its surface, which was a thin steel overlay on a wooden base, he saw a design of three golden lions alternating with three red hearts on a blue background.

A dim remembrance stirred in him. He stood puzzling for a while. Was this . . . wait. The Danish coat of arms. No, that had nine hearts. The memory sank down again.

But what in the world? He scratched his head. Had somebody been organizing a pageant, or what? He drew the sword: a great broad-bladed affair, cross-hilted, double-edged, and knife sharp. His engineer's eye recognized low-carbon steel. Nobody reproduced medieval equipment that accurately, even for a movie, let alone a parade. Yet he remembered museum exhibits. Man in the Middle Ages was a good deal smaller than his present-day descendants. This sword fitted his hand as if designed for that one grasp, and he was big in the twentieth century.

Papillon snorted and reared. Holger whirled around and saw the bear.

It was a large brown one, which had perhaps ambled around to investigate the noise. It blinked at them, Holger wished wildly for his gun, then the bear was gone again into the brush.

Holger leaned against Papillon till he got his wind back. "Now a small stand of wildwood is possible," he heard himself saying earnestly. "There may be a few hawks left. But there are no, positively no bears in Denmark."

Unless one had escaped from a zoo . . . He was going hog wild. What he must do was learn the facts, and cope with them.

Was he crazy, or delirious, or dreaming? Not likely. His mind was working too well by this time. He sensed sunlight and the fine dust motes which danced therein, leaves that formed long archways down the forest, the sharp mingled smells of horse and mold and his own sweat, everything utterly detailed and utterly prosaic. Anyway, he decided, as his naturally calm temperament got back into gear, he could do nothing but carry on, even in a dream. What he needed was information and food.

On second thought he reversed the order of importance.

The stallion seemed friendly enough. He had no right to take the beast, nor a suit of clothes, but his case was doubtless more urgent than that of whoever had so carelessly left this property here. Methodically he dressed himself; the unfamiliar stuff needed some figuring out but everything, to the very shoes, fitted disturbingly well. He repacked the extra garments and the armor and lashed them back in place. The stallion whickered softly as he swung himself up in the stirrups, and walked over to the lance.

"I never thought horses were that smart," he said aloud. "Okay, I can take a hint." He fitted the butt of the weapon into a rest he found depending from the saddle, took the reins in his left hand, and clucked. Papillon started sunward.

Not till he had been riding for some time did Holger notice how well he did so. His experience had hitherto been confined to some rather unhappy incidents at rental stables, and he recalled now having always said that a horse was a large ungainly object good only for taking up space that might otherwise be occupied by another horse. Odd, the instant affection he'd felt for this black monster. Still more odd, the easy way his body adjusted to the saddle, as if he'd been a cowboy all his life. When he thought about it, he grew awkward again, and Papillon snorted with what he could have taken oath was derision. So he pushed the fact out of his mind and concentrated on picking a way through the trees. Though they were following a narrow trail—made by deer?—it was a clumsy business riding through the woods, especially when toting a lance.

The sun went low until only a few red slivers showed behind black trunks and branches. Damn it, there just couldn't be a wild stretch this big anywhere in Denmark. Had he been carried unconscious into Norway? Lapland? Russia, for Pete's sake? Or had the bullet left him amnesiac, for weeks maybe? No, that wouldn't do. His injury was fresh.

He sighed. Worry couldn't stand against thoughts of food. Let's see, about three broiled cod and a mug of Carlsberg Hof . . . no, let's be American and have a T-bone, smothered in French-fried onions——

Papillon rested. He almost tossed Holger overboard. Through the brush and the rising darkness a lion came.

Holger yelled. The lion stopped, twitched its tail, rumbled in the maned throat. Papillon skittered and pawed the ground. Holger grew aware that he had dropped the lance shaft into a horizontal rest and was pointing it forward.

Somewhere sounded what could only be a wolf-howl. The lion stood firm. Holger didn't feel like disputing rights of way. He guided

Papillon around, though the horse seemed ready to fight. Once past the lion, he wanted to gallop; but a bough would be sure to sweep him off if he tried it in this murk. He was sweating.

Night came. They stumbled on. So did Holger's mind. Bears and wolves and lions sounded like no place on earth, except maybe some remote district of India. But they didn't have European trees in India, did they? He tried to remember his Kipling. Nothing came to him except vague recollections that east was east and west was west. Then a twig swatted him in the face and he turned to cursing.

"Looks as if we'll spend the night outdoors," he said. "Whoa."

Papillon continued, another shadow in a darkness that muttered. Holger heard owls, a remote screech that might be from a wildcat, more wolves. And what was that? An evil tittering, low in the brush—"Who's there? Who is that?"

Small feet pattered away. The laughter went with them. Holger shivered. It was as well to keep in motion, he decided.

The night had grown chilly.

Stars burst into his sky. He needed a moment to understand that they had emerged in a clearing. A light glimmered ahead. A house? He urged Papillon into a jarring trot.

When they reached the place, Holger saw a cottage of the most primitive sort, wattle and clay walls, a sod roof. Firelight was red on smoke rising from a hole in the top, and gleamed out the tiny shuttered windows and around the sagging door. He drew rein and wet his lips. His heart thumped as if the lion were back.

However . . .

He decided he was wisest to remain mounted, and struck the door with his lance butt. It creaked open. A bent figure stood black against the interior. An old woman's voice, high and cracked, came to him: "Who are ye? Who would stop with Mother Gerd?"

"I seem to be lost," Holger told her. "Can you spare me a bed?"

"Ah. Ah, yes. A fine young knight, I see, yes, yes. Old these eyes may be, but Mother Gerd knows well what knocks at her door o' nights, indeed, indeed. Come, fair sir, dismount ye and partake of what little a poor old woman can offer, for certes, ye've naught to fear from me, nor I from ye, not at my age; though mind ye, there was a time——But that was before ye were born, and now I am but a poor lonely old grandame, all too glad for news of the great doings beyond this humble cot. Come, come, be not afeared. Come in, I pray ye. Shelter is all too rare, here by the edge of the world."

Holger squinted past her, into the shack. He couldn't see anyone else. Doubtless he could safely stop here.

He was on the ground before he realized she had spoken in a language he did not know—and he had answered her in the same tongue.

2

HE SAT AT THE RICKETY TABLE of undressed wood. His eyes stung with
the smoke that gathered below the rafters. One door led into a stable
where his horse was now tied, otherwise the building consisted only of
this dirt-floored room. The sole dim light came from a fire on a hearth-
stone. Looking about, Holger saw a few chairs, a straw tick, some tools
and utensils, a black cat seated on an incongruously big and ornate
wooden chest. Its yellow gaze never winked or left him. The woman,
Mother Gerd, was stirring an iron pot above the fire. She herself was
stooped and withered, her dress like a tattered sack; gray hair straggled
around a hook-nosed sunken face which forever showed snaggle teeth
in a meaningless grin. But her eyes were a hard bright black.

"Ah, yes, yes," she said, " 'tis not for the likes of me, poor old
woman that I be, to inquire of that which strangers would fain keep hid.
There are many who'd liefer go a-secret in these uneasy lands near the
edge of the world, and for all I know ye might be some knight of Faerie
in human guise, who'd put a spell on an impertinent tongue. Nonetheless, good sir, might I make bold to ask a name of ye? Not your own
name, understand, if ye wish not to give it to any old dame like me,
who means ye well but admits being chattersome in her dotage, but
some name to address ye properly and with respect."

"Holger Carlsen," he answered absently.

She started so she almost knocked over the pot. "What say ye?"

"Why——" Was he hunted? Was this some weird part of Germany?
He felt the dagger, which he had prudently thrust in his belt. "Holger
Carlsen! What about it?"

"Oh . . . nothing, good sir." Gerd glanced away, then back to him,
quick and birdlike. "Save that Holger and Carl are both somewhat well-

known names, as ye wot, though in sooth 'tis never been said that one
was the son of the other, since indeed their fathers were Pepin and
Godfred, or rather I should say the other way around; yet in a sense, a
king is the father of his vassal and——"

"I'm neither of those gentlemen," he said, to stem the tide. "Pure
chance, my name."

She relaxed and dished up a bowl of stew for him, which he attacked
without stopping to worry about germs or drugs. He was also given
bread and cheese, to hack off with his knife and eat with his fingers,
and a mug of uncommonly good ale. A long time passed before he
leaned back, sighed, and said, "Thank you. That saved my life, or at
least my reason."

" 'Tis naught, sire, 'tis but coarse fare for such as ye, who must oft
have supped with kings and belted earls and listened to the minstrels of
Provence, their glees and curious tricks, but though I be old and humble,
yet would I do ye such honors as——"

"Your ale is marvelous," said Holger in haste. "I'd not thought to
find any so good, unless you——" He meant to say, "unless your local
brewery has escaped all fame," but she interrupted him with a sly laugh.

"Ah, good Sir Holger, for sure I am 'tis a knight ye must be, if not
of yet higher condition, ye're a man of wit and perceiving, who must
see through the poor old woman's little tricks on the instant. Yet though
most of your order do frown on such cantrips and call 'em devices of
the Devil, though in truth 'tis no different in principle from the wonder-
working relics of some saint, that do their miracles alike for Christians
or paynim, still must ye be aware how many here in this marchland do
traffic in such minor magics, as much for their own protection against
the Middle World powers as for comfort and gain, and ye can understand in your mercy 'twould scarce be justice to burn a poor old good-
wife for witching up a bit of beer to warm her bones of winter nights
when there be such many and powerful sorcerers, open traffickers in the
black arts, who go unpunished and——"

So you're a witch? thought Holger. *That I've got to see.* What did
she think she was putting over on him, anyway? What kind of buildup
was this?

He let her ramble on while he puzzled over the language. It was a
strange tongue, hard and clangorous in his own mouth, an archaic
French with a lot of Germanic words mixed in, one that he might have
been able to unravel slowly in a book but could surely never have
spoken as if born to it. Somehow the transition to—wherever this was—
had equipped him with the local dialect.

He had never gone in for reading romances, scientific or otherwise, but more and more he was being forced to assume that by some impossible process he had been thrown into the past. This house, and the carline who took his knightly accouterments as a matter of course, and the language, and the endless forest . . . But *where* was he? They had never spoken this way in Scandinavia. Germany, France, Britain? . . . But if he was back in the Dark Ages, how account for the lion, or for this casual mention of living on the boundaries of fairyland?

He thrust speculation aside. A few direct questions might help. "Mother Gerd," he said.

"Aye, good sir. With any service wherewith I can aid ye, honor falls on this humble house, so name your desire and within the narrow limits of my skill all shall be as ye wish." She stroked the black cat, which continued to watch the man.

"Can you tell me what year this is?"

"Oh, now ye ask a strange question, good sir, and mayhap that wound on your poor head, which doubtless was won in undaunted battle against some monstrous troll or giant, has addled messire's memory; but in truth, though I blush for the admission, such reckonings have long slipped from me, the more so when time is often an uncanny thing here in the wings of the world since——"

"Never mind. What land is this? What kingdom?"

"In sooth, fair knight, ye ask a question over which many scholars have cracked their heads and many warriors have cracked each other's heads. Hee, hee! For long have these marches been in dispute between the sons of men and the folk of the Middle World, and wars and great sorcerous contests have raged, until now I can but say that Faerie and the Holy Empire both claim it, while neither holds real sway, albeit the human claim seems a trifle firmer in that our race remains in actual settlement; and mayhap the Saracens could assert some title as well, forasmuch as their Mahound is said to have been an evil spirit himself, or so the Christians claim. Eh, Grimalkin?" She tickled the cat's throat.

"Well——" Holger clung to his patience with both hands. "Where can I find men . . . Christian men, let's say . . . who will help me? Where is the nearest king or duke or earl or whatever he is?"

"There is a town not too many leagues away as men reckon distance," she said, "yet in truth I must warn that space, like time, is wondrously affected here by the sorceries blowing out of Faerie, so that often the place where you are bound seems near, and then again dwindles into vast and tedious distances beset with perils, and the very land and way ye go remain not the same——"

Holger gave up. He knew when he was licked. Either this hag was a maundering idiot or she was deliberately stalling him. In neither case could he hope to learn much.

"Yet if 'tis counsel ye want," said Gerd suddenly, "though my own old noddle is oft woolly, as old heads are wont to be, and though Grimalkin here is dumb, however cunning, yet 'tis possible that counsel could be summoned for ye, and also that wherewith to allay your hurt and make ye whole again. Be not wroth, fair sir, if I propose a trifle of magic, for white it is—or gray, at worst; were I a mighty witch, think ye I would dress in these rags or dwell in this hovel? Nay, 'twould be a palace of gold for me, and servants on every hand would have welcomed ye. If by your leave I might summon a sprite, only a little one, he could tell ye what ye would know better than I."

"Hm." Holger raised his brows. All right, that settled it. She was nuts. Best humor her if he intended to spend the night here. "As you wish, mother."

"Now I perceive that ye hail from eldritch places indeed," she said, "for ye did not so much as cross yourself, whereas most knights are forever calling on the Highest, although oft in great oaths that will cost them hellfire pangs, nor live they overly godly lives; yet must the Empire use what poor tools can be found in this base and wicked world. Such is not your manner, Sir Holger, neither in one respect nor the other, which makes to wonder if indeed ye be not of Faerie. Yet shall we try this matter, though 'tis but right to confess beforehand the sprites are uncanny beings and may give no answer, or one with double meaning."

The cat sprang off the chest and she opened it. There was a curious tautness in her. He wondered what she was up to. A small crawling went along his spine.

Out of the chest she took a tripod brazier, which she set on the floor and charged with powder from a flask. She took out also a wand that seemed to be of ebony and ivory. Muttering and making passes, she drew two concentric circles in the dirt around the tripod and stood between them with her cat.

"The inner curve is to hold the demon, and the outer to stay what enchantments he might essay, for they are often grumpy when summoned so swift out of airiness," she explained. "I must ask ye, sir, to make no prayer nor sign of the cross, for that would cause him to depart at once, and in most foul humor too." Her voice was matter-of-fact, but her eyes glittered at him and he wished he could read expression in that web of wrinkles.

"Go ahead," he said, a bit thickly.

She began dancing around the inner circle, and he caught something of her chant. "*Amen, amen——*" Yes, he knew what was coming next, though he couldn't tell how he knew. . . . "—*malo a nos libera sed——*" Nor did he know why his hackles rose. She finished the Latin and switched to a shrill language he didn't recognize. When she touched her wand to the brazier, it began throwing out a heavy white smoke that almost hid her but, curiously, did not reach beyond the outer circle. "*O Beliya'al, Ba'al Zebub, Abaddon, Ashmadai!*" she screamed. "*Samiel, Samiel, Samiel!*"

Was the smoke thickening? Holger started from his chair. He could barely see Gerd in the red-tinged haze, and it was as if something else hovered over the tripod, something gray and snaky, half transparent— by Heaven, he saw crimson eyes, and the thing had almost the shape of a man!

He heard it speak, a whistling unhuman tone, and the old woman answered in the language he did not know. Ventriloquism, he told himself frantically, ventriloquism and his own mind, blurred with weariness, only that, only that. Papillon neighed and kicked in his stall. Holger dropped a hand to his knife. The blade was hot. Did magic, he gibbered, induce eddy currents?

The thing in the smoke piped and snarled and writhed about. It talked with Gerd for what seemed a very long time. Finally she raised her wand and started another chant. The smoke began to thin, as if it were being sucked back into the brazier. Holger swore shaken-voiced and reached for the ale.

When there was no more smoke, Gerd stepped out of the circle. Her face was gone blank and tight, her eyes hooded. But he saw how she trembled. The cat arched its back, bottled its tail, and spat at him.

"Strange rede," she said after a pause, tonelessly. "Strange rede the demon gave me."

"What did he say?" Holger whispered.

"He said—Samiel said ye were from far away, so far that a man might travel till Judgment Day and not reach your home. Is't not so?"

"Yes," said Holger slowly. "Yes, I think that may be true."

"And he said help for your plight, the means of returning ye whence ye came, lies within Faerie itself. There must ye go, Sir . . . Sir Holger. Ye must ride to Faerie."

He knew not what to answer.

"Oh, 'tis not so bad as 't sounds." Gerd eased a trifle. She even chuckled, or rather cackled. "If the truth must out, I am on terms not unfriendly with Duke Alfric, the nearest lord of Faerie. He is a kittle sort, like all his breed, but he'll help ye if ye ask, the demon said. And I shall furnish a guide, that ye may go thither with speed."

"Wh-why?" Holger stammered. "I mean, I can't offer payment."

"None is needed." Gerd waved a negligent hand. "A good deed may perchance be remembered to my credit when I depart this world for another and, I fear, warmer clime; and in any case it pleasures an old granny to help a handsome young man like unto ye. Ah, there was a time, how long ago——! But enough of that. Let me dress your hurt, and then off to bed with ye."

Holger submitted to having his injury washed and a poultice of herbs bound over it with an incantation. He was too tired by now to resist anything. But he remembered enough caution to decline her offer of her own pallet, and instead slept on the hay next to Papillon. No use taking more chances than he must. This was an odd house, to say the least.

3

WAKING, HE LAY for some time in a half doze, till he remembered where he was. Sleep drained from him. He sat up with a yell and glared around.

A stable, yes! A crude dark shelter, odorous with hay and manure, a black horse which loomed over him and nuzzled him tenderly. He climbed to his feet, picking straws out of his clothes.

Sunshine poured in as Mother Gerd opened the door. "Ah, good morrow, fair sir," she cried. "In truth ye slept the sleep of the just, or what's said to be the sleep of the just, though in my years I've oft espied good men tossing wakeful the night through and wicked men shaking the roof with their snores; and I'd not the heart to waken ye. But come now and see what waits."

That proved to be a bowl of porridge, more bread and cheese and ale, and a hunk of half-cooked bacon. Holger consumed the meal with appetite and afterward thought wistfully of coffee and a smoke. But wartime shortages had somewhat weaned him from those pleasant vices. He settled for a vigorous washing at a trough outside the cottage.

When he came back in, a newcomer had arrived. Holger didn't see him till a hand plucked at his trousers and a bass voice rumbled, "Here I be." Looking down, he saw a knotty, earth-brown man with jug-handle ears, outsize nose, and white beard, clad in a brown jacket and breeches, with bare splay feet. The man was not quite three feet tall.

"This is Hugi," said Mother Gerd. "He'll be your guide to Faerie."

"Ummm . . . pleased to meet you," said Holger. He shook hands, which seemed to astonish the dwarf. Hugi's palm was hard and warm.

"Now be off with ye," said the old woman cheerily, "for the sun is high and ye've a weary way to go through realms most parlous. Yet fear not, Sir Holger. Hugi is of the woods-dwellers and will see ye safe to Duke Alfric." She handed him a cloth-wrapped bundle. "Herein have I laid some bread and meat and other refreshment, for well I know how impractick ye young paladins are, gallivanting about the world to rescue fair maidens with never a thought of taking along a bite of lunch. Ah, were I young again, 'twould matter naught to me either, for what is an empty belly when the world is green, but now I am aged and must think a bit."

"Thank you, my lady," said Holger awkwardly.

He turned to go. Hugi pulled him back with surprising strength. "What's the thocht here?" he growled. "Would ye gang oot in mere cloth? There's a mickle long galoots in yon woods were glad to stick iron in a rich-clad wayfarer."

"Oh . . . oh, yes." Holger unwrapped his baggage. Mother Gerd sniggered and hobbled out the door.

Hugi assisted him to put on the medieval garments properly, and bound leather straps about his calves while he slipped the padded undercoat over his head. The ringmail clashed as he pulled it on next, and hung with unexpected weight from his shoulders. Now, let's see—obviously that broad belt went around his waist and carried his dagger, while the baldric supported his sword. Hugi handed him a quilted cap which he donned, followed by the Norman helmet. When gilt spurs were on his feet and a scarlet cloak on his back, he wondered if he looked swashbuckling or plain silly.

"Good journey to ye, Sir Holger," said Mother Gerd as he walked outside.

"I . . . I'll remember you in my prayers," he said, thinking that would be an appropriate thanks in this land.

"Aye, do so, Sir Holger!" She turned from him with a disquieting shrill laughter and vanished into the house.

Hugi gave his belt a hitch. "Come on, come on, ma knichtly loon, let's na stay the day," he muttered. "Who fares to Faerie maun ride a swift steed."

Holger mounted Papillon and gave Hugi a hand up. The tiny man hunkered down on the saddlebow and pointed east. "That way," he said. " 'Tis a twa-three days' ganging to Alfric's cot, so off we glump."

The horse fell into motion and the house was soon lost behind them. The game trail they followed today was comparatively broad. They rode under tall trees, in a still green light that was full of rustlings and birdcalls, muted hoofbeats, creak of leather and jingle of iron. The day was cool and fair.

For the first time since waking, Holger remembered his wound. There was no ache. The fantastic medication had really worked.

But this whole affair was so fantastic that—— He thrust all questions firmly back. One thing at a time. Somehow, unless he was dreaming (and he doubted that more and more; what dream was ever so coherent?) he had fallen into a realm beyond his own time, perhaps beyond his whole world: a realm where they believed in witchcraft and fairies, where they certainly had one genuine dwarf and one deucedly queer creature named Samiel. So take one thing at a time, go slow and easy.

The advice was hard to follow. Not only his own situation, but the remembrance of home, the wondering what had happened there, the hideous fear that he might be caught here forever, grabbed at him. Sharply he remembered the graceful spires of Copenhagen, the moors and beaches and wide horizons of Jutland, ancient towns nestled in green dales on the islands, the skyward arrogance of New York and the mist in San Francisco Bay turned gold with sunset, friends and loves and the million small things which were home. He wanted to run away, run crying for help till he found home again—no, none of that! He was here, and could only keep going. If this character in Faerie (wherever *that* might be) could help him, there was still hope. Meanwhile, he could be grateful that he wasn't very imaginative or excitable.

He glanced at the hairy little fellow riding before him. "You're kind to do this," he ventured. "I wish I could repay you somehow."

"Na, I do 't in the witch's service," said Hugi. "No that I'm boond to her, see ye. 'Tis but that noo and oftimes some o' us forest folk help her, chop wood or fetch water or run errands like this. Then she does for us in return. I canna say I like the old bat much, but she'll gi' me mickle a stoup o' her bra bricht ale for this."

"Why, she seemed . . . nice."

"Oh, ah, she's wi' a smooth tongue when she wills, aye, aye." Hugi chuckled morbidly. " 'Twas e'en so she flattered young Sir Magnus when he came riding, many and many a year ago. But she deals in black arts. She's a tricksy un, though no sa powerful, can but summon a few petty demons and is apt to make mistakes in her spells." He grinned. "I recall one time a peasant in the Westerdales did gi' her offense, and she swore she'd blight his crops for him. Whether 'twas the priest's blessing he got, or her own clumsiness, I know na, but after long puffing and striving, she'd done naught but kill the thistles in his fields. Ever she tries to curry favor wi' the Middle World lords, so they'll grant her more power, but thus far she's had scant gain o' 't."

"Ummm——" That didn't sound so good. "What happened to this Sir Magnus?" asked Holger.

"Oh, at the last, crocodiles ate him, methinks."

They rode on in silence. Eventually Holger asked what a woods dwarf did. Hugi said his people lived in the forest—which seemed of enormous extent—off mushrooms and nuts and such, and had a working arrangement with the lesser animals like rabbits and squirrels. They had no inherent magical powers, such as the true Faerie dwellers did, but on the other hand they had no fear of iron or silver or holy symbols.

"We'll ha' naught to do wi' the wars in this uneasy land," said Hugi. "We'll bide our ain lives and let Heaven, Hell, Earth, and the Middle World fight it oot as they will. And when you proud lairds ha' laid each the other oot, stiff and stark, we'll still be here. A pox on 'em all!" Holger got the impression that this race resented the snubs they had from men and Middle Worlders alike.

He said hesitantly, "Now you've made me unsure. If Mother Gerd means no good, why should I follow her advice and go to Faerie?"

"Why, indeed?" shrugged Hugi. "Only mind, I didna say she was always evil. If she bears ye no grudge, she micht well ha' ta'en the whim to aid ye in truth. E'en Duke Alfric may help, just for the fun in such a new riddle as ye seem to offer. Ye canna tell wha' the Faerie folk will do next. They canna tell theirselves, nor care. They live in wildness, which is why they be o' the dark Chaos side in this war."

That didn't help a bit. Faerie was the only hope he had been given of returning home, and yet he might have been directed into a trap. Though why anyone should bother to trap a penniless foreigner like himself——

"Hugi," he asked, "would you willingly lead me into trouble?"

"Nay, seeing ye're no foe o' mine, indeed a good sort, no like some I could name." The dwarf spat. "I dinna know what Mother Gerd has in mind, nor care I overmuch. I've told ye what I do know. If ye still want to gang Faeriewards, I'll guide ye."

"And what happens then is no concern of yours, eh?"

"Richt. The wee uns learn to mind their ain affairs."

Bitterness edged the foghorn bass. Holger reflected that it might be turned to his own ends. He wasn't altogether a stranger to people with overcompensated inferiority complexes. And surely Hugi could give more help than simply guiding him into he knew not what.

"I'm thirsty," he said. "Shall we stop for a short snort?"

"A short what?" Hugi wrinkled his leathery face.

"Snort. You know, a drink."

"Snort . . . drink. . . . Haw, haw, haw!" Hugi slapped his thigh. "A guid twist, 'tis. A short snort. I maun remember 't, to use i' the woodsy burrows. A short snort!"

"Well, how about it? I thought I heard something clink in that bundle of food."

Hugi smacked his lips. They reined in and untied the witch's gift. Yes, a couple of clay flasks. Holger unstoppered one and offered Hugi the first pull, which surprised the dwarf. But he took good advantage of it, his Adam's apple fluttering blissfully under the snowy beard, till he belched and handed the bottle over.

He seemed puzzled when they rode on. "Ye've unco manners, Sir Holger," he said. "Ye canna be a knicht o' the Empire, nor e'en a Saracen."

"No," said Holger. "I'm from rather farther away. Where I come from, we reckon one man as good as the next."

The beady eyes regarded him closely from beneath shaggy brows. "An eldritch notion," said Hugi. "Hoo'll ye steer the realm if commons may sup wi' the gentle?"

"We manage. Everybody has a voice in the government."

"But that canna be! 'Tis but ane babble then, and naught done."

"We tried the other way for a long time, but leaders born were so often weak, foolish, or cruel that we thought we could hardly be worse off. Nowadays in my country the king does little more than preside. Most nations have done away with kings altogether."

"Hum, hum, 'tis vurra strange talk, though in truth——why, this makes me think ye maun be o' the Chaos forces yerselves."

"What do you mean?" asked Holger respectfully. "I'm ignorant of your affairs here. Could you explain?"

He let the dwarf growl on for a long time without learning much. Hugi wasn't very bright, and a backwoodsman as well. Holger got the idea that a perpetual struggle went on between primeval forces of Law and Chaos. No, not forces exactly. Modes of existence? A terrestrial reflection of the spiritual conflict between heaven and hell? In any case, humans were the chief agents on earth of Law, though most of them were so only unconsciously and some, witches and warlocks and evil-doers, had sold out to Chaos. A few nonhuman beings also stood for Law. Ranged against them was almost the whole Middle World, which seemed to include realms like Faerie, Trollheim, and the Giants—an actual creation of Chaos. Wars among men, such as the long-drawn struggle between the Saracens and the Holy Empire, aided Chaos; under Law all men would live in peace and order and that liberty which only Law could give meaning. But this was so alien to the Middle Worlders that they were forever working to prevent it and to extend their own shadowy dominion.

The whole thing seemed so vague that Holger switched the discussion to practical politics. Hugi wasn't much help there either. Holger gathered that the lands of men, where Law was predominant, lay to the west. They were divided into the Holy Empire of the Christians, the Saracen countries southward, and various lesser kingdoms. Faerie, the part of the Middle World closest to here, lay not far east. This immediate section was a disputed borderland where anything might happen.

"In olden time," said Hugi, "richt after the Fall, nigh everything were Chaos, see ye. But step by step 'tis been driven back. The longest step was when the Saviour lived on earth, for then naught o' darkness could stand and great Pan himself died. But noo 'tis said Chaos has rallied and mak's ready to strike back. I dinna know."

Hm. There was no immediate chance to separate fact from fancy. But this world paralleled Holger's own in so many ways that some connection must exist. Had fleeting contact been made from time to time, castaways like himself who had returned with stories that became the stuff of legend? Had the creatures of myth a real existence here? Remembering some of them, Holger hoped not. He didn't especially care to meet a fire-breathing dragon or a three-headed giant, interesting as they might be from a zoological standpoint.

"Oh, by the bye," said Hugi, "ye'll have to leave yer crucifix, if ye bear one, and yer iron at the gates. Nor may ye speak holy words inside. The Faerie folk canna stand against sic, but if ye use 'em there, they'll find ways to send ye ill luck."

Holger wondered what the local status of an agnostic was. He had, inevitably, been brought up a Lutheran, but hadn't been inside a church for years. If this thing must happen to somebody, why couldn't it have been a good Catholic?

Hugi talked on. And on. And on. Holger tried to pay friendly attention, without overdoing the act. They got to telling stories. He dug out every off-color joke he could remember. Hugi whooped.

They had stopped by a moss-banked stream for lunch when the dwarf abruptly leaned forward and put a hand on Holger's arm. "Sir Knicht," he said, looking at the ground, "I'd fain do ye a guid turn, if ye wish."

Holger kept himself steady with an effort. "I could use one, thanks."

"I dinna know wha' the best coorse be for ye. Mayhap 'tis to seek Faerie e'en as the witch said, mayhap 'tis to turn tail richt noo. Nor have I any way to find oot. But I ken ane i' the woods, a friend to all its dwellers, who'd know any news abroad in the land and could belike gi' ye a rede."

"If I could see him, that would be a . . . a big help, Hugi."

" 'Tis no a him, 'tis a her. I'd no tak' any other knicht thither, for

they're a lustful sort and she likes 'em not. But ye . . . well . . . I canna
be an evil guide to ye."

"Thank you, my friend. If I can ever do you a service——"

" 'Tis naught," growled Hugi. "I do 't for ma ain honor. And watch
yer manners wi' her, ye clumsy loon!"

4

THEY TURNED NORTHWARD and rode for several hours, most of which Hugi spent reminiscing about his exploits among the females of his species. Holger listened with one ear, pretending an awe which was certainly deserved if half the stories were true. Otherwise he was lost in his own thoughts.

As they entered higher country the forest became more open, showing meadows full of wildflowers and sunlight, gray lichenous boulders strewn between clumps of trees, now and then a view across hills rolling into purple distance. Here were many streams, leaping and flashing in their haste to reach the lower dales, rainbows above them where they fell over the bluffs. Kingfishers flew there like small blue thunderbolts, hawks and eagles soared remotely overhead, a flock of wild geese rose loud from the reeds of a mere, rabbits and deer and a couple of bears were seen in glimpses. White clouds swept their shadows across the uneven many-colored land, the wind blew cool in Holger's face. He found himself enjoying the trip. Even the armor, which had dragged at first, was become like a part of him. And in some dim way there was a homelikeness about these lands, as if he had known them once long before.

He tried to chase down the memory. Had it been in the Alps, or in Norway's high *saetere*, or the mountain meadows around Rainier? No, this was more than similarity. He almost knew these marches of Faerie. But the image would not be caught, and he dismissed it as another case of *déjà vu*.

Though if his transition here had taught him a new language, it might well have played other tricks with his brain. For a moment he had a wild idea that perhaps his mind had been transferred to another body. He looked down at his big sinewy hands and reached up to touch the familiar dent in the bridge of his nose, souvenir of that great day when he helped clobber Polytech 36 to 24. No, he was still himself. And, incidentally, in rather bad need of a shave.

The sun was low when they crossed a final meadow and halted under trees on the shore of a lake. The water caught the light and became a sheet of fire a mile across; a flock of brant whirred from the rushes. "We can wait here," said Hugi. He slid to the ground and rubbed his buttocks. "Oof," he grimaced, "ma puir auld backside!"

Holger dismounted as well, feeling a certain aftereffect himself. No reason to tether the doglike Papillon; he looped the bridle up and the stallion began contentedly cropping. "She'll arrive soon, belike," rumbled Hugi. " 'Tis her ain nest hereaboots. But whilst we wait, laddie, we could be refreshing oorselves."

Holger took the hint and broke out the ale. "You still haven't told me who 'she' is," he said.

" 'Tis Alianora, the swan-may." Beer gurgled down the dwarf's throat. "Hither and yon she flits throughout the wood and e'en into the Middle World sometimes, and the dwellers tell her their gossip. For she's a dear friend to us. Aaaaah! Auld Mother Gerd, a witch she may be, but a brewmistress beyond compare!"

Papillon neighed. Turning, Holger saw a long form of spotted yellow glide toward the lake. A leopard! His sword was out and aloft before he knew it.

"Nay, nay, hold." Hugi tried to grab his arm, couldn't reach far enough, and settled for his legs. "He comes in peace. He'll no set on ye unless ye offer ill to the swan-may."

The leopard flowed to a halt, sat down, and watched them with cool amber eyes. Holger sheathed his blade again. Sweat prickled him. Just when these wilds were becoming familiar, something like this had to happen.

Wings beat overhead. " 'Tis she!" cried Hugi. He jumped about, waving his arms. "Hallo, there, hallo, come on doon!"

The swan fluttered to earth a yard away. It was the biggest one Holger had ever seen. The evening light burned gold on its plumage. He took an awkward step forward, wondering how you introduced yourself to a swan. The bird flapped its wings and backed away.

"Nay, nay, be naught afeared, Alianora." Hugi darted between. "He's a bra sire who'd but ha' speech wi' ye."

The swan stopped, poised, spread its wings wide and stood on tiptoe. Its body lengthened, the neck shrank, the wings narrowed—*"Jesu Kriste!"* yelled Holger and crossed himself. A woman stood there.

No, a girl. She couldn't be over eighteen: a tall slender young shape, lithe and sun-browned, with bronze-colored hair loose over her shoulders, huge gray eyes, a few freckles across a pert snub nose, a mouth wide and gentle—why, she was beautiful! Almost without thought, Holger slipped his chinstrap free, doffed helmet and cap, and bowed to her.

She approached shyly, fluttering long sooty lashes. Her only garment was a brief tunic, sleeveless and form-fitting, that seemed to be woven of white feathers; her bare feet were soundless in the grass. "So 'tis ye, Hugi," she said, with more than a hint of the dwarf's burr in her soft contralto. "Welcome. Also ye, Sir Knight, sith ye be a friend to my friend."

The leopard crouched, switched its tail and gave Holger a suspicious look. Alianora smiled and went over to chuck it under the chin. It rubbed against her legs, purring like a Diesel engine.

"This long lad hight Sir Holger," said Hugi importantly. "And as ye see, my fere, yon be the swan-may hersel'. Shall we sup?"

"Why——" Holger sought for words. "It's a pleasure to meet you, my lady." He was careful to use the formal pronoun; she was timid of him, and the leopard was still present. "I hope we haven't disturbed you."

"Och, nay." She smiled and relaxed. "The pleasure be mine. I see so few folk, sairly gallant knichts." Her tone had no particular coquetry, she was only trying to match his courtliness.

"Ah, let's eat," growled Hugi. "Ma belly's a-scraping o' ma backbane."

They sat down on the turf. Alianora's teeth ripped the tough dark bread Holger offered as easily as the dwarf's. No one spoke until they had finished, when the sun was on the horizon and shadows had grown as long as the world. Then Alianora looked directly at Holger and said: "There be a man seeking of ye, Sir Knicht. A Saracen. Is he friend o' yours?"

"Ah, a, a Saracen?" Holger pulled his jaw back up with a click. "No. I'm a, a stranger. I don't know any such person. You must be mistaken."

"Mayhap," said Alianora cautiously. "What brocht ye here unto me, though?"

Holger explained his difficulty, whether or not to trust the witch. The girl frowned, a tiny crease between level dark brows. "Now that, I fear, I canna tell," she murmured. "But ye move in darksome company, Sir Knicht. Mother Gerd is no a good soul, and all know how tricksy Duke Alfric be."

"So you think I'd best not go to him?"

"I canna say." She looked distressed. "I know naught o' the high ones in Faerie. I only ken a few o' the lesser folk in the Middle World, some kobolds and *nisser*, a toadstool fay or two, and the like."

Holger blinked. There they went again. No sooner had he begun to imagine he was sane, in a sane if improbable situation, than off they were, speaking of the supernatural as if it were part of everyday.

Well . . . maybe it was, here. Damnation, he'd just seen a swan turn into a human. Illusion or not, he didn't think he could ever have seen that in his own world.

The initial shock and the inward numbness it brought were wearing off. He had begun to realize, with his whole being, how far he was from home, and how alone. He clenched his fists, trying not to curse or cry.

To keep his mind engaged, he asked, "What did you mean about a Saracen?"

"Oh, him." The girl looked out across the twilit glimmer of the lake. Swallows darted and swooped out there, amid an enormous quietness. "I've no seen him mysel', but the woods be full o' the tale, moles mumble it in their burrows and the badgers talk o' it to the otters, then kingfisher and crow get the word and cry it to all. So I hear that for many weeks now, a lone warrior, who must by his face and garb be a Saracen, has ridden about these parts inquiring after a Christian knicht he believes to be nigh. He's no said why he wanted the man, but the aspect o' him, as the Saracen relates, is yours: a blond giant on a black horse, bearing arms o'——" She glanced toward Papillon. "Nay, your shield is covered. The device he speaks of be three hearts and three lions."

Holger stiffened. "I don't know any Saracens," he said. "I don't know anyone here. I come from farther away than you understand."

"May this be an enemy o' yers, seeking ye oot to slay?" asked Hugi, interested. "Or a friend, e'en?"

"I tell you, I don't know him!" Holger realized he had shouted. "Pardon me. I feel all at sea."

Alianora widened her eyes. "All at sea? Oh, aye." Her chuckle was a sweet sound. "A pretty phrase."

Somewhere in the back of his mind, Holger recorded the fact for future use that the clichés of his world seemed to pass for new-coined wit here. But mostly he was busy thinking about the Saracen. Who the devil? The only Moslem he'd ever known had been that timid, bespectacled little Syrian at college. Under no circumstances would *he* have gone around in one of these lobster get-ups!

He, Holger, must have made off with the horse and equipment of a man who, coincidentally, resembled him. That could mean real trouble. No point in seeking out the Saracen warrior. Most certainly not.

A nihilistic mood of despair washed over him. "I'll go to Faerie," he said. "I don't seem to have any other chance."

"And a chancy place 'tis for mortals," said Alianora gravely. She leaned forward. "Which side be ye on? Law or Chaos?"

Holger hesitated. "Ha' no fear," she urged. "I stand at peace wi' most beings."

"Law, I suppose," he said slowly, "though I don't know a thing of this wor—— this land."

"I thocht so," said Alianora. "Well, I'm human too, and even if the minions o' Law be often guzzling brutes, I think still I like their cause better than Chaos. So I'll gang alone wi' ye. It may be I can give ye some help in the Middle World."

Holger started to protest, but she raised a slender hand. "Nay, nay, speak no o' it. 'Tis scant risk for me who can fly. And——" She laughed. "And it could be a richt merry adventure, methinks!"

Night was coming, with stars and dew. Holger spread his saddle blanket to sleep in, while Alianora went off saying she'd rather house in a tree. The man lay awake for a long time to watch the constellations. They were familiar, the late summer sky of northern Europe up there. But how far away was home? Or had distance any meaning?

He recalled that when Alianora changed into the human form, he had unthinkingly crossed himself. He'd never done so before in his life. Was it just the effect of this medieval environment, or part of the unconscious skills, language and riding and Lord knew what else, he had somehow gained? It was lonely, not even knowing yourself.

There were no mosquitoes here. For small blessings give praises. But he might have welcomed one, as a reminder of home.

Finally he slept.

5

THEY SET OUT in the morning, Holger and Hugi on Papillon. Alianora flew overhead as a swan, curving and soaring and vanishing behind the trees to reappear in an upward swoop. The man's spirits rose with the sun. If nothing else, he was bound somewhere, and seemed to be in good company. By noon their eastward course brought them high in the hills, a rough windy land of scarred boulders, waterfalls and ravines, long harsh grass and gnarled copses. To Holger's eye the horizon ahead looked darker than it should.

Hugi broke into hoarse bawdy song. To match him, Holger rendered such ballads as "The Highland Tinker" and "The Bastard King of England," translating with an ease that surprised himself. The dwarf guffawed. Holger had begun *"Les Trois Orfévres"* when a shadow fell on him and he looked up to see the swan circling above, listening with interest. He choked.

"Eigh, do go on," urged Hugi. " 'Tis a rare bouncy song."

"I've forgotten the rest," said Holger weakly.

He dreaded facing Alianora when they stopped for lunch. That was by a thicket which shielded a cave mouth. The girl came lightly toward him in human form. "Ye've a tuneful way wi' ye, Sir Holger," she smiled.

"Ummmm . . . thank you," he mumbled.

"I would ye could recollect wha' happened to the three goldsmiths," she said. " 'Twas rude o' ye to leave them there on the rooftop."

He stole a look at her. The gray eyes were wholly candid. Well, if she'd spent her life among the earthy little people— He didn't have the nerve, though. "I'll try to remember," he said falsely.

The brush rustled behind them and they saw a creature emerge from the cave. At first Holger thought it was deformed, then he decided it must be a normal member of a nonhuman race. The body was somewhat taller than Hugi and much broader, with muscular arms hanging to the bent knees; the head was big and round, flatnosed, with pointed ears and a gash of a mouth; the skin was hairless and gray. "Why, 'tis Unrich," cried Alianora. "I thocht no ye denned this far upland."

"Oh, Ay git aroon, Ay do." The being hunkered down and regarded Holger with circular eyes. He wore only a leather apron, and carried a hammer. "We-un bin a-drayvin' a new shaft thisaboots." He waved at the surrounding territory. "Thar's gold in them thar hills."

"Unrich belongs wi' the nickels," explained Alianora. Holger concluded that must be a tribe of mountain dwarfs rather than a class of coins or a series of alloys. "I got to ken him through the badger families."

The newcomer was as avid for gossip as everyone here seemed to be. Holger's tale must be recounted from the beginning. At the end the nickel shook his head and spat. " 'Tis naw so canny a steadin' ye're boon fawr," he said. "An' roight noo, too, when the Middle World is marshalin' all uns hosts."

"Aye," said Hugi, " 'tis a cold welcome we micht get at Alfric's."

"They do say elves an' trolls ha' made allayance," said Unrich. "An' when them thar clans get together, 'tis suthin' big afoot."

Alianora frowned. "I mislike this," she said to Holger. "Sorceries go ever more boldly abroad, even into the heart o' the Empire, I hear. 'Tis as if a bulwark o' Law has been taken away, so that Chaos can freely flow out over the world."

"That wuz a holy spell put on Cortana, but noo 'tis berried away fro' soight o' man, an' none able to wield it were it dug up," said Unrich with a certain pessimistic relish.

Cortana, thought Holger. Where had he heard that name before?

Unrich reached in a pocket of his apron and, to Holger's surprise, drew out a stubby clay pipe and a sack of something that looked like tobacco. Striking fire with flint and steel, he inhaled deep. Holger watched wistfully.

"That's a dragonish trick, yon fire-breathing," said Hugi.

"Ay loike un," said Unrich.

"And quite rightly, too," said Holger. " '—a woman is only a woman, but a good Cigar is a Smoke.' "

They stared at him. "I ne'er heard o' mankind playing demon thus," said Alianora.

"Lend me a pipe," said Holger, "and see!"

"This is too guid to miss." Unrich ducked back in his cave and returned presently with a large briar. Holger tamped, got a light, and blew happy clouds. He didn't think he was smoking tobacco, it was strong as the very devil, but no worse than stuff he'd had in France before the war or Denmark during. Hugi and Unrich goggled at him. Alianora went into peals of laughter.

"How much do you want for this?" asked Holger. "I'll swap you a spare cloak for the pipe, with flint and steel and a pouch of tobac—— of smoking-leaf."

"Done!" said Unrich at once. Holger realized he could have made a better bargain. Oh, well.

"Ye micht have the decency to throw in some food for us," said Alianora.

"Wull, sith 'tis yew what ask." Unrich disappeared again. Alianora looked commiseratingly at Holger. "Ye men are scarce a practick breed," she sighed.

With a load of bread, cheese, and smoked meat they set off again. Though the country grew yet steeper and wilder, Papillon seemed tireless. The gloom in the east rose before them as they proceeded, like a vague wall. Near evening, they halted at what must be the crest of the range; below, the thinly begrown hills swooped down toward pine woods. Alianora set deftly to work building a shelter of plaited withes, while Hugi prepared supper and Holger felt useless. But he enjoyed watching the girl move about.

"Tomorrow," she said, as they sat around the fire after nightfall, "we'll enter Faerie. After that, 'tis in the hands o' fate."

"What makes it so dark in that direction?" asked Holger.

Alianora stared at him. "Truly ye're from afar off, or else a spell is on ye," she said. "All folk know the Pharisees canna endure broad daylight, so 'tis forever twilit in their realm." She winced. The firelight etched her young face redly against wind-whining blackness. "If Chaos wins, mayhap yon dusk will be laid on the whole world, and no more o' bricht sunshine and green leaves and blossoms. Aye, I suppose indeed I am with Law." She paused. "And yet does Faerie have an eldritch beauty. Ye'll see for yoursel'."

Holger looked across the blaze at her. The light shone in her eyes, stroked her hair and the gentle curves of her body, then wove her a mantle of shadow. "If I am not being rude," he ventured. "I can't understand why a pretty girl like you should live in the wilds among . . . among others than your own kind."

"Oh, 'tis no hard riddle." She gazed into the coals. He could barely hear her voice above the night wind. "The dwarfs found me as a babe lying in the forest. Belike I was some crofter's child, stolen in the harrying which ever goes through these marches. The robbers thought to raise me for a slave, then wearied o' the idea and left me. So the little folk, and the animals their oath-brethren, raised me up. They were good and kind, and they taught me a mickle. In the end they gave me this swan dress, which they say once belonged to the Valkyries. By its power, I, though not shapestrong born but o' common human sort, may change as ye've seen; and thus I may dwell safe. Now go whither ye will, said the dwarfs. But I couldna care much for the smoky halls o' men. My friends were here, and the space and sky I maun have to be glad. That is the whole o' 't."

Holger nodded, slowly.

She glanced back at him. "But ye've told us only a whit about yoursel'," she said with an unsteady smile. "Where be your home, and how came ye hither without traversing lands o' men or Middle World and learning wha' they were?"

"I wish I knew," said Holger.

He wanted to tell her the whole story, but thrust the impulse back. She probably couldn't understand any part of it. Besides, he might be wise to have some secrets in reserve. "I think a spell was laid on me," he said. "I lived so far off that we'd never heard of any of these places. All at once, here I was."

"What micht your realm be called?" she insisted.

"Denmark." He swore at himself when she exclaimed:

"But I've heard o' yon kingdom! Though far from here, it has a wide fame. A Christian country, north o' the Empire, is 't no?"

"Ummm . . . well . . . that can't be the same Denmark." Hardly! "Mine lies in—ah——" He hated to tell her an outright falsehood. Wait a minute; his old junkets around the United States. "I am thinking of a place in South Carolina."

She cocked her head at him. "Methinks ye're hiding summat. Well, as ye wish. We border folk learn not to be overcurious." She yawned. "Shall we to bed?"

They huddled together in the shelter, seeking warmth as the night grew more cold. Several times Holger wakened with a shiver and sensed Alianora breathing by his side. She was a sweet kid. If he never found his way back——

6

THEIR DESCENT next morning was rapid, if precarious. Often Hugi yelped as Papillon's hoofs slipped on the talus and they teetered over a blowing edge of infinity. Alianora stayed far overhead. She had a hair-raising sport of turning human in midair and going back to swan shape just in time to break her fall. After watching this Holger needed a steadying smoke quite badly. He couldn't light the pipe until Hugi showed him how to use the flint and steel he now carried in the pouch at his belt. Damnation, why couldn't they have matches in this world?

As they went through the pine wood, the twilight closed in like stormclouds. It deepened with every muffled step. Holger wondered whether they would be able to see at the end of the trip. His scalp prickled at the thought of groping blind through a country of trolls and werewolves and God knew what else.

The air grew warmer as they descended. When at length they emerged from the forest, the atmosphere was balmy, laden with incense-like odors of blossoms unknown to Holger. They entered an open, roll-ing valley, and Hugi gulped. "Noo we be within Faerie," he muttered. "Hoo we gang oot again be another tale."

Holger swept the landscape with a wondering look. Though the sun was hidden, the night he had feared was not fallen. He could identify no source of light, but saw almost as clearly as by day. The sky was a deep dusky blue, and the same blueness pervaded the air as if he rode under water. Grass grew long and soft, with a silvery hue overlying its pale green; white flowers starred the earth. *Asphodels*, Holger thought. But how did he know? Here and there he saw bushes of white roses. Trees stood alone and in copses, tall, slim, milky of bark, their leaves the color of the grass. The slow wind blew through them with a tiny ringing sound. He couldn't gauge their distances well in this tricky shadowless light. A brook ran close by which did not tinkle but played, an endless melody on an alien scale. Phosphorescence eddied white and green and blue over the water.

Papillon snorted and shuddered. He didn't like this place.

But where have I seen it before, just such a cool calm blue over wan trees and hills that melt into sky, where else has the wind blown thus singingly and the river chimed like bells of glass? Was it in a dream once long ago, half sleeping and half waking in the light summer night of Denmark, or was it in a year older and forgotten? I do not know. I do not think I wish to know.

They rode on. In that changeless luminance, time seemed fluid and unstable, so that they might have traveled for a minute or a century, but the vague landscape slipped past them and still they rode. Until the swan came rushing down again, landed with a thunder of wings and became Alianora.

There was fear on her face. "I saw a knicht bound hither," she said breathlessly. "A knicht o' Faerie. What he would, I canna tell."

Holger felt his heart begin a heavy thumping, but he held his outward appearance calm. "We'll find out."

The stranger came over a ridge. He bestrode a tall horse, snowy white, with flowing mane and proudly arched neck; yet the beast was subtly wrong to look at, too long of leg, too small of head. The rider was in full plate armor, his visor down so that he showed no face; white plumes nodded on the helmet, his shield was blank and black, all else shimmered midnight blue. He halted and let Holger approach him.

When the Dane was close, the knight lowered his lance.

"Stand and declare yourself!" His voice had a resonant, metallic quality, not quite human.

Holger reined in. Papillon whickered on a defiant note. "I was sent by the witch Mother Gerd with a message for Duke Alfric."

"First let me see your arms," called the brass voice. "Hither come none unknown."

Holger shrugged, to disguise his own unease. Reaching down, he unbuckled the shield where it hung and slipped it on his left arm. Hugi pulled off the canvas cover. "Here you are."

The Faerie knight reared back his horse, spurred, and charged.

"Defend yersel'!" shrieked Hugi. He tumbled off the saddle. "He's after yer life!"

Papillon sprang aside while Holger still gaped. The other horseman went past with a dull drumming of hoofs. He wheeled and came back, the spearhead aimed at Holger's throat.

Blind reflex, then. Holger lowered his own lance, kicked Papillon, and lifted his shield to guard himself. The black stallion sprang forward. The enemy shape grew terribly close. His lance dipped toward Holger's midriff. The Dane brought his own shield down and braced feet in stirrups.

They hit with a bang that sent echoes from hill to hill. Holger's shield was jarred back against his stomach. He almost lost his lance as it caught the opponent's visor. But the other shaft splintered, and the Faerie knight lurched in the saddle. Papillon pressed ahead. The stranger went over his horse's tail.

He was on his feet at once, incredible that he could do so in full armor, and his sword hissed free. There was still no time to think. Holger had to let his body act for him, it knew what to do. He hewed at the dismounted enemy. Sword belled on sword. The Faerie knight hacked at Holger's leg. The Dane turned the blow just in time. He himself crashed blade down on the plumed helmet. Metal rang aloud, and the foeman staggered.

Too clumsy, striking from above. Holger leaped to the ground. His foot caught in a stirrup and he went flat on his back. The stranger sprang at him. Holger kicked. Again that brazen clash; the warrior fell. Both scrambled up. The newcomer's glaive clattered on Holger's shield. Holger cut at the neck, trying to find an open joint in the plates. The Faerie warrior chopped low, seeking his unprotected legs. Holger skipped back. The other rushed at him, sword blurred with speed. Holger parried the blow in mid-air. The shock jarred in his muscles. The Faerie blade spun free. At once the stranger drew a knife and leaped close.

The broadsword wasn't meant for thrusting, but Holger saw a crack above the gorget before him and stabbed inward. Sparks poured forth. The metal form reeled, sank to its knees, fell to the grass with a last rattle, and lay still.

Dizzily, a roar in his ears, Holger looked about. He saw the white horse fleeing eastward. *Off to tell the Duke*, he thought. Then Hugi was dancing and cheering around him, while Alianora clung to his arm and sobbed and exclaimed how splendidly he had done battle.

I? he thought. *No, that wasn't me. I don't know a thing about swords and lances.*

But who, then, won this fight?

Alianora bent over the fallen shape. "He's no bleeding," she said huskily. "Yet belike he is slain, for the Pharisees canna endure touch o' cold iron."

Holger took a long breath. His mind began to clear. He saw his mistakes; yes, he should have stayed mounted and used his horse as a secondary weapon. He'd take better care next time. Briefly he wondered what the Faerie dwellers—Pharisees, as they seemed to be called, doubtless because an illiterate human population had gotten its Biblical references confused—he wondered what they used in place of steel. Aluminum alloys? Surely magic could extract aluminum from bauxite. Beryllium, magnesium, copper, nickel, chromium, manganese——

While doubtless correct, the idea of an elvish wizard with a spectroscope was funny enough to restore a balance in Holger. He startled his comrades by laughing aloud. "Well," he said, a bit astonished at his own callousness, "let's see what we've got."

He knelt and opened the visor. Hollowness gaped at him. The armor was empty. It must have been empty all the time.

7

FAERIE SEEMED A WILDERNESS, hills and woods and uncultivated valleys. Holger asked a much subdued Hugi what its inhabitants lived on. The dwarf explained that they magicked up some of their food and drink, and got some from other realms in the Middle World tributary to them, and hunted some among the weird beasts which prowled their domain. All of them seemed to be warriors and sorcerers, their menial work done by slaves taken from the goblins, kobolds, and other backward tribes. Further questions revealed that the Pharisees knew not old age or illness, but were said to lack souls. They would not be the most pleasant company imaginable, Holger thought.

Trying to find solid mental ground and forget that hollow armor lying in the field of asphodels, he began to theorize. He had only a fair knowledge of physics and mathematics, but he should be able to make some intelligent guesses. There had to be a rationale for this world!

Both the similarities to home, such as the constellations, and the differences, such as now encompassed him, ruled out the possibility of another planet in space. In the same space as his own, that is. The ordinary laws of nature, like gravity and chemical combination, appeared to obtain; but here they apparently had clauses permitting, well, magic. Conceivably the magic was nothing but a direct control of matter. Even where he came from, some people believed in telepathy, telekinesis, and so forth. In this world, under certain conditions, mental forces could perhaps be stronger than inorganic ones. . . . He had gotten thus far when he realized that he had gotten nowhere, merely given a different name to the same set of phenomena.

Well, be that as it may, *where* was he? Or should he ask *when* was he? Another Earth? Maybe two objects could occupy the same space at the same time without interacting with each other. Which meant two entire starry universes could. Any number of universes. He had fallen into one such: one so parallel to his own—in spite of the differences—that there must be some link between them. How?

He sighed and gave up. First things first. Right now he had to keep alive in a land where a good many beings had it in for one who bore three hearts and three lions.

The castle grew slowly out of twilight. Its walls rose dizzily high, the roofs all peaks and angles, overtopped with soaring thin towers: a wild beauty, like ice on a winter forest. The white stone seemed lacy, so fragile that a breath would dissolve it, but as he approached Holger saw how massive the walls were. A moat surrounded the hill on which the castle stood, and though no river emptied therein, the water circled endlessly chiming.

Not far away stood another hill, covered with roses, half hidden by streamers of mist, but seeming to have the shape of a woman's breast. Hugi pointed to it. "Yon's Elf Hill," he said, very low. "Inside there do the elves hold their unco revels, and come oot o' 't to dance o' moonlicht nichts." In the background, a forest so dark that Holger could scarcely see individual trees stretched north, south, and east. "There in Mirkwood do the Pharisee lairds hunt griffin and manticore," whispered Hugi.

A trumpet sounded from the castle, far and cold, like rushing water. *Now they've seen us*, Holger thought. He dropped a hand to his sword. Alianora fluttered down to turn human beside him. Her expression was grave.

"You and Hugi——" He cleared his throat. "You've guided me here, and I thank you a thousand times. But now perhaps you'd best go."

She looked up at him. "Nay," she said after a moment, "I think we'll stay a bit. Mayhap we can help ye."

"I'm no one to you," he faltered. "You don't owe me a thing, while I owe you more than I can ever repay."

The gray eyes remained serious. "Methinks ye're summat more than no one, e'en if ye dinna ken it yoursel'," she murmured. "I've a feeling about ye, Sir Holger. So I, at least, will stay."

"Well," puffed Hugi, though not so happily, "ye didna think I'd turn caitiff noo, did ye?"

Holger didn't urge them. He'd done his duty, offering them an excuse to leave; and God, was he glad they hadn't taken it!

The castle gates opened and the drawbridge came down, noiselessly. Trumpets blew again. A troop rode forth with banner and scutcheon, plume and lance, to meet him. He reined in and waited, his hand tight around his own spear. So these were the masters of Faerie.

They were clad in colors that seemed luminous against the twilight, crimson, gold, purple, green, but the hue of each garment shimmered and flickered and changed from moment to moment. Some wore chain mail or plate, argent metal elaborately shaped and chased; others had robes and coronets. They were a tall people, moving with a liquid grace no human could rival, nor even a cat. A cold haughtiness marked their features, which were of a strange cast, high tilted cheekbones, winged nostrils, narrow chin. Their skin was white, their long fine hair blue-silver, most of the men beardless. When they got close enough, Holger thought at first they were blind, for the oblique eyes held only an azure blankness. But he soon realized their vision was better than his.

The leader halted and bowed a little in his stirrups. "Welcome, Sir Knight," he said. His voice was beautiful to hear, more like song than speech. "I hight Alfric, Duke of Alfarland in the Kingdom of Faerie. 'Tis not oft that mortal men come to guest us."

"Thank you, my lord." The polished phrases fell of themselves from Holger's lips. "The witch Mother Gerd, who I believe is a humble servant of yours, commended me to your grace. She thought belike your wisdom could solve a grief of mine, so hither I came to beg the favor."

"Ah, so. Well met, then. I bid you and your servitors remain for as long as it pleasures you, and shall strive to aid a gentleman of your standing with what power I may have."

My standing? Holger reflected that the thing which attacked him was undoubtedly a creature of the Duke's. Three hearts and three lions didn't seem at all popular in the Middle World. The question was, did Alfric now understand that Holger wasn't the man he had wanted killed? And whether he knew it or not, what went on behind that smooth chill face?

"I thank your grace," said Holger aloud.

"It pains me that I must bid you leave cross and iron outside, but you know the unfortunate weakness of our race," said Alfric urbanely. "Fear not, you shall be given arms in exchange."

"In your stronghold, my lord, can be nothing to fear," said Holger and thought what a liar he was becoming.

Alianora shifted from foot to small foot. "I'll watch your stuff, Holger," she said. "I'd liefer stay outdoors anyway."

Alfric and the other Pharisees turned their wide blank eyes on her. " 'Tis the swan-may of whom we have heard," smiled the Duke. "Nay, fair damsel, we would be ill hosts did we not offer you too a roof."

She shook her ruddy head stubbornly. A frown touched Alfric's brow. "Wouldst not refuse?" he breathed.

"Wouldst," snapped Alianora.

"I'll abide oot here wi' her," said Hugi quickly.

"Nay, go ye with Sir Holger," said the girl.

"But——" said Hugi.

"Ye heard me," said Alianora.

Alfric shrugged. "If you wish to join us, Sir Knight——" he hinted.

Holger climbed down and doffed his armor. The Pharisees looked away when he touched his cross-hilted weapons. Papillon snorted and glared at their horses. Alianora loaded the equipment on the stallion and took his bridle. "I'll await ye in the woods," she said, and led the charger off. Holger's eyes followed her till she had disappeared.

The party trooped into the stronghold. A courtyard stretched wide, with arbors and flowerbeds and splashing fountains, with music and a heavy smell of roses on the air. Before the main keep Holger saw the ladies of Faerie gathered to watch. For a while he forgot everything else. *Jumping Judas!* It was worth crossing universes just to get a look. He bowed to them in a daze.

Alfric told a short, green-skinned goblin slave to lead him to his quarters. "We will await you at dinner," he said graciously. Holger, with Hugi trotting in his wake, passed along labyrinthine corridors, high and vaulted and dimly gleaming. Through arched doorways he glimpsed rooms ablaze with jewels. Of course, he thought, trying to maintain equilibrium, when you could conjure such things from the air——

Up a long, curved flight of stairs, down another hall, into a suite of rooms right out of the Arabian Nights. The goblin kowtowed and left them. Holger looked around at glowing carpets, mosaics of precious stones, cloth-of-gold hangings, out balcony windows to acres of garden. Tapers burned with a clear unwavering light. On one wall hung a tapestry whose figures slowly changed, acting out a story from which he looked away with a slight shiver.

"I maun say they do theirselves richt well here," declared Hugi. "Natheless, I'd swap the whole caboodle to be back under ma ain auld oak root. Here's a tricksy bigging."

"No argument." Holger wandered into a bathroom which offered him every comfort of home, soap, hot running water, scissors, razor, a glass mirror, and yet was like nothing from home. Nevertheless he came out feeling much refreshed. On the bed lay a suit which must be meant for him; when he donned it, he was fitted as if with another skin. Full-sleeved silken shirt, purple satin vest, crimson hose, short blue mantle, black velvet shoes, everything worked with gold thread and jewels,

trimmed with soft strange furs, boosted his morale still higher. He noticed a set of military gear in a corner, including a sword with a crescent-
shaped guard. That was tactful of Alfric, though one could scarcely
carry weapons to dinner.

"Och, 'tis a bra figure ye cut, Sir Holger," admired Hugi. "Belike
ye maun fight off the Faerie dames. They're lickerish lot here, 'tis said."

"I wish I knew why everyone's turned so friendly," said Holger.
"Aren't the Pharisees on uneasy terms with mankind, at best? Why
should Alfric put himself out like this for me?"

"No telling, lad. Mayhap 'tis but a snare for ye. Then again, it may
amuse him to do ye a kindness. Ye canna guess wha' the Faerie folk
will think or do. They know not theirselves, nor care."

"I feel guilty about letting you sit here and Alianora camp out in
the woods."

"Oh, they'll gi' me summat t' eat, and the lassie's happier where
she be. I ken what's in her mind. I'm t' help ye wi' rede and deed
herein, whilst she waits ootside to do wha' she can if need should arise."

A goblin appeared, to announce obsequiously that dinner was
served. Holger followed him down smoky-blue halls and into a chamber
so huge he could scarcely see the end or the ceiling. The lords and
ladies of Faerie surrounded the table like a melted rainbow. Unhuman
slaves scurried about, music came from somewhere, talk and laughter
danced above a somehow unbroken hush.

Holger was conducted to Alfric's left, with a girl introduced as
Meriven on his other side. The impact of her face and figure was such
that he scarcely heard the name. Rubber-kneed, he sat down and tried
to make conversation.

She responded readily, despite the feebleness of his efforts. From
what he overheard Holger gathered that talk was a high art here: swift,
witty, poetic, cynical, always a hint of delicate malice, always with
elaborate rules he didn't begin to comprehend. Well, he thought, im-
mortals who had nothing to do but hunt, magic, intrigue, and wage war,
would develop sophistication out of sheer necessity. They hadn't heard
of forks here, but the food and the many wines were a symphony. If
only Meriven weren't so distracting. This was a classic *embarras de
richesses.*

"Truly," she breathed, holding his gaze with those curious eyes that,
in her, no longer bothered him, "you are a bold man thus to venture
hitherwards. That death-stroke you gave your foe, ah, 'twas beautiful!"

"You saw?" he asked sharply.

"In the Black Well, yes. I watched you. As to whether we but jested,
or intended your life in earnest, Sir 'Olger, 'tis not good for a young

man to know too much. A trace of puzzlement keeps him from stodginess." She laughed sweetly. "But what does bring you here?"

He grinned. "Nor should a young lady know too much," he answered.

"Ah, cruel! Yet am I glad you came." She used the intimate pronoun. "I may address you thus, fair sir? There is a kinship of spirit between us, even if we find ourselves at war now and again."

"Dearest enemy," said Holger. She drooped her lids, smiling with appreciation. His own eyes had a tendency to fall too—that décolletage of hers. He searched his mind for more cribs from Shakespeare. The situation was made to order.

They continued the flirtation throughout the banquet, which seemed to take hours. Afterward the company went into an even larger chamber for dancing. But as the music started, Duke Alfric drew Holger aside.

"Come with me a moment, if you will, good sir," he said. "We'd best talk over your problem at once, under four eyes, so that I can think on it awhile; for I foresee that our ladies will give you scant peace."

"Thank you, your grace," said Holger, a trifle grumpily. He didn't much care to remember realities just now.

They strolled into a garden, found a bench beneath a luminous willow, and sat down. A fountain danced before them, a nightingale sang behind. Alfric's black-clad body leaned back in one supple motion. "Say what you will, Sir 'Olger," he invited.

Well, no use holding anything back. If the Pharisee did have power to return him, he'd probably have to know the whole situation. Only where to start? How do you describe an entire world?

Holger did his best. Alfric guided him with occasional penetrating questions. The Duke never showed surprise, but at the end he seemed thoughtful. He leaned elbows on knees and drew the knife of white metal which he carried at his waist. As he turned it over and over, Holger read the inscription upon the blade. *The Dagger of Burning*. He wondered what that meant.

"A strange tale," said Alfric. "I have never heard one more strange. Yet methinks there is truth in it."

"Can . . . can you help me?"

"I know not, Sir 'Olger—for so it still seems natural to call you. I know not. There are many worlds in space, as any sorcerer or astrologue is aware, but a plurality of universes is another concept, only darkly hinted in certain ancient writings. If I heard you without being made helpless by amazement, 'tis because I have myself speculated that another Earth such as you describe might indeed exist, and be the source of myths and legends, such as those told of Frederik Barbarossa, or the

great epical chansons about the Emperor Napoleon and his heroes." As
if to himself, Alfric murmured a few lines:

> *"Gerard li vaillant, nostre brigadier magnes,*
> *tres ans tut pleins ad esté an Espagne*
> *combattant contre la Grande-Bretagne."*

He shook himself and went on more briskly: "I shall raise spirits
which can give counsel. No doubt that will take time, but we shall strive
to show you hospitality. I think we have good hope of ultimate success."

"You are much too kind," said Holger, overwhelmed.

"Nay." Alfric waved his hand. "You mortals know not how tedious
undying life can become, and how gladly a challenge such as this is
greeted. 'Tis I should thank you."

He rose, chuckling. "And now, methinks you'd fain return to the
dance," he said. "Good pleasance, my friend."

Holger returned in a haze of joy. He'd been too quick to judge this
Middle World. No one could have been more kind or courteous than
the Pharisees. He liked them!

Meriven headed off several other ladies as he entered the ballroom.
She pounced on his arm and said archly, "I know not why I do this, Sir
Knight. Off you went, with never a word, and left me forsaken."

"I'll try to make up for that," he said.

The elfin music surrounded him, entered him. He didn't know the
stately figure dances he saw, but Meriven caught on to the fox trot at
once; he'd never had a better partner. He wasn't sure how long the ball
lasted. They slipped out into the garden, drank from a fountain of wine,
laughed, and did not return. The rest of the night was as much fun as
any he had ever spent, or rather more so.

8

HERE THERE WAS no real morning or evening, day or dark; the dwellers seemed to live according to whim. Holger woke slowly and luxuriously, to find himself alone again. At exactly the right moment the door opened and a goblin entered with a breakfast tray. They must have used witchcraft to learn his personal tastes: no Continental nonsense, but a good American assemblage of ham and eggs, toast, buckwheat cakes, coffee, and orange juice. By the time he was up and dressed, Hugi came in, looking worried. "Where were you?" asked Holger.

"Ah, I slept in the garden. It seemed the richt thing to do when ye were, uh, busy." The dwarf sat down on a footstool, an incongruous brown blot in this gold and scarlet and purple. He tugged at his beard. "I dinna like the air here. Summat ill is afoot."

"You're prejudiced," said Holger. Mostly he was thinking of a date he'd made to go hawking with Meriven.

"Och, they can put on a bra show and bedazzle ye wi' every manner o' fine wines and loose lasses," grumbled Hugi, "but there's aye been scant friendship atwixt men and Faerie, least of all noo when Chaos gathers for war. As for me, I ken wha' I ken. And this is what I spied as I lay in yon garden. Great flashes o' lightning from the topmost tower, a demon figure departing in smoke, and the stench o' warlockry so rank it nigh curdled ma banes. Later, from the west, another flying figure came in haste, landed on the tower and went inside. Methinks Duke Alfric ha' summoned a weirdie to his aid."

"Why, of course," said Holger. "He told me he would."

"Have yer fun," muttered Hugi. "Be gay in the teeth o' the wolf. But when yer dead body lies oot for ravens to tear, say no I didna warn ye."

A stubborn objectivity forced Holger to consider the dwarf's words as he went downstairs. Indeed this might be a gimmick to keep him out of commission until too late. . . . Too late for what? Surely, if they intended evil, they could stab or poison him. He'd stood off one of their champions—who had probably only attacked him because he bore the arms of the mysterious paladin of the hearts and lions—but he couldn't beat a dozen. Could he? He dropped hand on the Faerie sword. It was a comforting thing to have.

Meriven hadn't set a definite hour, here where time hardly existed. Holger dawdled through the main reception hall. After a while he thought he might look up the Duke and ask if there was any news about his problem. On inquiry from a sullen kobold slave, Holger learned that the master's rooms were in the north wing, second floor. He mounted a flight of stairs three at a bound, whistling cheerily.

He came out on the landing just as Alfric and a woman stepped from a door. He had barely a glimpse of her, she slipped swiftly back inside again, but he was stunned. This world seemed full of extraordinary lookers. She was human, taller and more full-bodied than the Faerie ladies, long midnight hair coiled under a golden coronet, her white satin dress sweeping the floor. Her face was ivory pale, curve-nosed, with arrogance lying on the red lips and in the dark brilliant eyes. Hm! The Duke was a lucky fellow.

Alfric's scowl smoothed itself out. "Good morrow, Sir 'Olger. How fare you?" As he bowed, his hands moved in curious passes.

"Excellent well, my lord." Holger bowed back. "I trust you too——"

"Ah, there you are, my naughty one. Wouldst run away from me?" Meriven took the Dane's arm. Now where the devil had she appeared from? "Come, the horses are ready, we've some falconry to do." She bore him off almost before he could draw breath.

They had a good time, loosing their hawks at cranes, wild peacocks, and less familiar prey. Meriven chattered gaily the while, and he had to laugh with her. That anecdote about the hunting of the basilisk . . . well, hardly fit for mixed company, but it was funny. Holger would have enjoyed himself more had his memory not been nagging him again. That woman with the Duke—blast and damn, he *knew* her!

He'd only had a flying look, but the image remained sharp within him; he knew her voice would be low and her manner haughty, capricious, sometimes kind and sometimes cruel, but all her moods no more than an iridescence on the surface of an intransigent will. Meriven seemed rather pallid compared to . . . to . . . what was her name?

"You're sad, my lord." The Pharisee girl laid a hand on his.

"Oh, no. No. I was only thinking."

"Fie on you! Come, let me make a charm to drive thought away, 'tis the child of care and the father of sorrow." Meriven pulled a green twig off a tree, bent it, and gestured with some words. It became an Irish harp, which she played while singing him love songs. They did lull him most pleasantly, but——

As they neared the castle again, she caught his arm and pointed. "Nay, see!" she hissed. "A unicorn! They've become rare hereabouts."

He glimpsed the beautiful white beast flitting between the trees. A stray wisp of ivy had caught on its horn. Wait. He peered through the half-light. Didn't someone walk beside it?

Meriven tensed pantherishly. "If we steal close——" she whispered. Her horse moved forward, hoofs noiseless on the turf.

The unicorn stopped, looked back at them, and was away, a shining shadow rapidly lost to sight. Meriven swore with unladylike imaginativeness. Holger said nothing, because he had seen what accompanied the animal. For one moment he had locked eyes with Alianora. Now she was also gone.

"Well, lackaday, such is life." Meriven came back to him and they rode on together. "Be not so downcast, my lord. Mayhap we can make a party later and run the brute down."

Holger wished he were more of an actor. He mustn't let her guess his own suddenly mounting suspicions. At the same time, he had to think them through. It wasn't that he had any new reason to think badly of Faerie: just the sight of Alianora had triggered something in him. He needed Hugi's counsel.

"If you will forgive me, my lady," he said, "I'll go bathe before dinner."

"Oh, my bath is large enough for us both, and for some fine sports I can teach you," she offered.

Holger wished he had a helmet to cover his ears. They felt incandescent. "I'd like a short nap, too," he said clumsily. Inspiration: "I must be at my best for you later on. There's so much competition."

He beat a retreat before she could insist, and almost ran to his apartments. Hugi looked up from the bed, on which he had curled himself. Holger bent over the dwarf.

"I saw a woman this morning," he said, fast and softly; and he described her, not from the bare glance he had had but from a memory which seemed to stretch over many years. "Who is she?"

"Why——" Hugi rubbed his eyes. "That sounds like ye've spied Queen Morgan le Fay. Could it ha' been hersel' whom Alfric summoned last nicht from Avalon? Then there's deviltry abroad for fair."

Morgan le Fay! That was it. Holger knew so with a certainty beyond knowledge. And Avalon, yes, he had seen an island of birds and roses, rainbows and enchantment, but where and when and how? "Tell me about her," he urged. "Everything you know."

"Ho, is 't yon doxy ye noo hanker for? She's na for the likes o' ye, lad, nor e'en for Duke Alfric. Cast no yer eyes too high up, lest the sun blind 'em. Or better, lest the moon strike ye mindless."

"No, no, no! I have to know, that's all. Maybe I can figure out why she's here."

"Well, noo . . . I dinna ken mickle. Avalon lies far, far in the western ocean, a part o' the world wha' we've nobbut auld wives' tales aboot here. Hooever, folk know Morgan le Fay is sister to Arthur, the last great king o' the Britons, though in her the Faerie strain in yon family runs strong and wild. She's the michtiest witch in Christendie or heathendom, and could belike match hersel' wi' aught in the Middle World. Immortal, she is, and a kittle un; none know if she stands wi' Law or Chaos or only her ain self. 'Tis said she bore off Arthur when he lay grievous wounded, to heal him and keep him against his time to return. Yet could be that were but a sly excuse to hold him from just such a coming back. Och, I'm no gleeful to be under ane roof wi' her."

Still no proof. Morgan might have come here to help Alfric on Holger's problem, or she might have stopped in on some altogether unrelated errand. But it did look queer.

A goblin entered the bedchamber. "The good Duke gives a feast for castle servants," he said. "You, dwarf, are bidden."

"Ummm——" Hugi tugged his beard. "I thank ye, nay. I dinna feel so well."

The goblin raised his hairless brows. " 'Twill be taken ill if you spurn the feast," he said.

Hugi traded a look with Holger. The man nodded. Maybe this was a device to get the dwarf out of the way, but if so, there didn't seem to be any means of evading it. "Go on," he said. "Have a good time."

"Aye, so. Take care o' yersel'." Hugi trotted after the goblin. Holger lit his pipe and lay down in the bath which had drawn itself for him, to think. He felt as if he were caught in spider webs. Very delicate, very lovely, but you couldn't get out. For a panicky moment, he wanted to shout and run.

He suppressed the feeling. He could do nothing at present but string along. And his suspicions were based on so little. Still——

A new suit of party clothes was laid out for him. He donned it, the laces and buckles fastening themselves. Hardly had he finished when the doorknob formed into metallic lips and said politely, "His grace the Duke asks leave to enter your presence."

"Yipe!" said Holger. Recovering himself: "P-p-please come in." Evidently slaves, being beneath notice, came and went without asking, while the upper classes respected each other's privacy.

The Pharisee entered, his chiseled white visage smiling. "I bring good news," he said. "I have conferred with numerous of the Powers, and there seems to be an excellent chance of sending you back home."

"Why . . . why . . . I cannot thank you, your grace," Holger stammered.

" 'Twill take some time to gather the necessities for the spells," Alfric said. "Meanwhile, methinks a special merrymaking is called for. There's to be an entertainment in Elf Hill."

"Hm? Oh, yes. I've seen the place."

Alfric took his arm. "Shall we away, then? I warrant you'll have some lusty hours. The elves know how to make a man glad."

Holger didn't feel like an orgy, but had no way to refuse. They went down the stairs. The castle dwellers were gathering, a murmurous swirl of color through the halls and out into the courtyard. Meriven trod forth from among them, and Alfric relinquished Holger to her.

"I'll accompany you into the hill," she said. "I've no mind to let some elvish hussy steal you."

"Why, isn't everyone coming?" he asked.

"Presently. You and I are to go in first. The others will follow later. You shall see how 'tis planned."

Holger thought of death traps and dismissed the notion, since one of their own would be with him.

The procession wound out of the gates, over the bridge, across the lawns toward Elf Hill of the roses. Behind him curveted warriors on horseback, banners flying from their lances, musicians playing horns and harps and lutes, a hundred lords and ladies of Faerie, who danced as they neared the mound. And now Holger heard music which rose to answer theirs, a skirling sweetness that entered his blood and roiled in his head. He smiled down at Meriven, all at once eager, and she laughed back and hung close on his arm. Her loose pale hair blew up across his face, half blinding him, the perfumes like a taste of strong wine. The hill opened. Through Meriven's tresses he glimpsed wavering lights, against which tall figures stood black. The music hurried his feet for him, he couldn't wait.

Hoofbeats hammered in the earth. A horse neighed, loud and angry. Holger whirled to see Alianora on Papillon, galloping out of the woods. Her face was distorted with terror.

"Holger! Nay, Holger, not in there!"

9

BEHIND HIM ALFRIC SHOUTED a curse. A spear flashed through the air, hardly missing the girl. Holger stood locked in amazement. "Get him in the hill!" yelled Alfric.

Meriven pulled at his arm. Three Pharisee men plunged forward like football tackles. A sudden rage snapped up into Holger. He launched himself to meet them. The nearest he stiff-armed, letting him drop with a grunt and lie quietly. His right fist swung around, trailing Meriven, and smashed another handsome face. The third warrior he dodged. A horseman loomed before him, lance almost in his ribs. He tore the grimly clinging Meriven loose, lifted her above his head, and pitched her at the rider's midriff. Both went over the horse's crupper.

Three chevaliers had closed in on Alianora. Papillon reared, struck out with his forefeet, and sent one clattering from the saddle. Whirling, the huge black stallion bit a chunk out of the next Faerie horse, which screamed and bolted. The third rider slashed at Alianora. She ducked his sword and sprang to the ground.

"Hai!" She had leaped almost into the arms of a velvet-clad Pharisee lord. He grabbed her, grinning as she tried to writhe free. But then he held a swan. And swans have vicious tempers.

"Yi!" he shouted as she pecked at his eyes. "Yee!" he added as a wing-buffet nearly broke his jaw. "Help!" he finished when she nipped off a finger, and dropped her and fled.

The Faerie lords boiled around Holger, hewing and thrusting at his unarmored body. He was too excited to feel any hurts. A remote part of him wondered at the incredible luck which was letting him by with minor flesh wounds. Could it be luck? He fed the nearest enemy a mouthful of knuckles, snatched the fellow's sword, and hacked around him. The blade was lighter than iron, he could swing it one-handed, but the edge was keen. An axman cut at his bare head. He caught the haft with his free hand, wrenched it loose, and waded into the Pharisees with ax and sword.

Papillon attacked the crowd from behind, kicking, biting, trampling, till he reached Holger. The man's foot found a stirrup. He vaulted up. The stallion was off in a gallop.

Hoofs thudded behind. Turning his head, Holger saw the mounted knights bear down on him. Their animals were even faster than his. He had dropped his captured weapons and Alianora had perforce abandoned his lance. Reaching down, he got sword and shield where they hung. There was scarcely time to put on the armor bundled behind his saddle.

The swan winged white beside him. Suddenly she swerved. An eagle struck where she had been. Holger looked up and saw more great birds descending from the sky. *Oh, my God, they're turning themselves into eagles, they'll get her now——*

Alianora hissed, beat a way with wings and beak past two of them, and streaked for the forest. Turned human again, she could find shelter from the ornithomorphs in the dense brake. But how then could she go fast enough to escape ground pursuit?

A horse drew alongside Papillon. Alfric himself bestrode it, a sword in one hand. His long silvery hair streamed from a face that still smiled. Loud through hoofbeats, cloven air, and the hunting horns blowing in the ear came his shout: "So let us try if indeed you are invincible, Sir 'Olger du Danemark!"

"Gladly!" snarled the Dane. Alfric was on his unshielded right side, but he was past caring. His sword hammered down, meeting the lighter Faerie blade in mid-air. Alfric's weapon darted aside, in past Holger's guard. With skill he had not known was his, Holger got his edge under the crescent-shaped hilt of the enemy and threw the strength of his shoulders against Alfric's hand. The Duke's weapon was torn from his grasp. He snarled and pulled his horse closer, so his knee touched Holger's as they galloped. His left hand shot out, snake-swift, closing on the Dane's sword wrist. He couldn't hold his bigger opponent long; but he needed little time to draw the knife at his belt.

Holger twisted in his own seat. He couldn't quite interpose his shield, but he brought its edge down on Alfric's dagger hand. The Duke screamed. Smoke spurted from his skin. Holger caught the smell of singed flesh. The white horse stampeded. By Heaven, it was true what they said! The Faerie metabolism could not endure the touch of iron.

Holger reined in Papillon so clods jumped underfoot. Turning, he reared the stallion, waved his sword and howled at the riders: "All right, come and get it! Step right up and lay right down!"

They stopped as swiftly as he had done, milling aside. But through the twilight, Holger saw warriors who ran toward him on foot, carrying bows. That wasn't so good. They could stand afar and fill him with arrows. Recklessly, he plunged toward them with some idea of breaking up the formation. "Rah, rah, rah!" he shouted. *"Ti-i-iger!"*

The knights scattered before his charge. The bowmen stood their ground. He heard a shaft buzz nastily by his ear. *"Jesu Kriste Fili Mariae——"*

The Pharisees shrieked! They spurred their horses, threw away their weapons, ran and galloped from him like an explosion. So it was also true they couldn't stand to hear a holy name, thought Holger exultantly. He should have remembered that. Only . . . why had his unthinking appeal been in Latin?

He was tempted to throw the whole hierarchy after them, but decided not to abuse his privilege. An honest prayer was one thing; taking the Great Names in vain for mere advantage was something else again, and could bring no luck. (How did he know that? Well, he did.) He settled for steering Papillon back westward and shouting, "Hi-yo, Silver!"

After all, the story was that the Faerie folk didn't like silver either.

Something gleamed in the trampled grass. He stopped his horse, leaned far over, and picked up the knife Duke Alfric had dropped. It didn't seem formidable, not very sharp, feather-light in his hand; yet the blade was inscribed *The Dagger of Burning*. Puzzled, vaguely hopeful that it might be a useful talisman, he thrust the weapon in his belt.

Now, Alianora. He trotted along the fringe of the woods, calling her name, but there was no answer. His exuberance died within him. If she had been killed—hell's fire, he thought with stinging eyes, it wasn't that he would be alone in this world of enemies, it was that she was a grand kid and had saved his life. And how had he repaid her? he asked himself glumly. What sort of friend was he, guzzling and swilling and making up to alien women while she lay in the cold dew and——

"Alianora!"

No answer. No sound whatsoever. The wind had laid itself to rest, the castle was hidden in swiftly rising mists, the forest was a wall of night. Nothing save the fog moved, nothing spoke, he was the only thing alive in all this dimness. He thought uneasily that he couldn't linger here. The Pharisees would soon figure out some way to get at him. They could summon allies who were not bothered by iron or God. Morgan le Fay, for instance. If he meant to escape, he'd better do so at once.

He rode westward along the forest boundary, calling for Alianora. Still the fog deepened, lifting from the ground in white banks and streamers, muffling the sound of Papillon's hoofs, seeming almost to smother his own breath. Drops glistened in the horse's mane; his shield glimmered wet. The world closed in till he could hardly see two yards.

A *Faerie stunt*, he thought with a gulp of fear. They could blind him this way; thereafter he should be easy to overcome. He urged Papillon into a canter. Despite the dank chill, his mouth was dry.

Something loomed ahead, vague and pale in the curling grayness. "Hallo!" he yelled. "Who's there? Stand or I'll have at you!"

Laughter answered, not the wicked snickering of Faerie but clear and young. " 'Tis only me, Holger. I had to mount myself. We could scarce ride double the long way we must gang, and my wings would grow weary."

She came into sight, a brown slim figure in white feather-tunic. Dewdrops twinkled in her hair. She was riding a unicorn bareback, doubtless the same one he had spied earlier. It regarded him with wary onyx eyes and wouldn't come near. Mounted before the girl was the hunched form of Hugi.

"I doubled back to fetch this lad," she explained, "and then we went into the woods again and I whistled up my steed. But ye'll have to take him now, for 'twas all I could do to make Einhorn carry anyone but me even so small a way."

Holger felt thoroughly ashamed. He had quite forgotten Hugi. And a peeved Duke Alfric would probably have made short work of the dwarf. He took the little man from Alianora's arms and set him on his own saddlebow.

"Now what should we do?" he asked.

"Noo we maun galumph quick's may be oot o' this ill realm," grunted Hugi. "Sooner we're in honest lands, better oor chances be o' living to brag aboot this dunce's trip."

"Hm, yes. Though I'm afraid we'll get lost in the fog."

"I'll fly above from time to time to get bearings," Alianora said. "Thus we'll outtrick them who conjured it up."

They trotted on through the wet soundless murk. Holger began to feel the reaction to battle. It took the shape of a conviction of his own worthlessness. What was he good for, except to drag fine resourceful people like Alianora into peril of their lives? What had he done, even, to earn the food he'd eaten so far? He was the merest pensioner, a bumbling idiot kept alive by charity.

He remembered a question that had touched his mind. "Hugi," he asked, "why was it dangerous for me to go into that hill?"

"Know ye na this?" The dwarf raised his thick brows. "So yon's why they lured me from ye! So I couldna give warning. . . . Well, then, know that time is strange inside Elf Hill. They'd ha' held ye there wi' one nicht o' merrymaking, and when ye came oot again, a hundred years would ha' passed here. In the meanwhile the Middle Worlders would ha' been able to do whate'er 'tis ye noo stand in the way o'."

Holger shuddered.

But this did throw a new light on his own status. It was unthinkable that Alfric and Morgan could have continued to mistake him for some champion whose arms he bore. Therefore he himself, Holger Carlsen, orphan and exile, *he* was in some way a focal point of the gathering crisis. How, he couldn't imagine. Possibly his coming from another universe gave him—what? An aura? At any rate, the forces of Chaos had to win him to their side or, failing that, get him out of their way.

The lavish hospitality, including Meriven, had obviously been an essay at the first. It had also served to hoodwink him while Alfric summoned Morgan le Fay and conferred with her. Evidently they had decided to take no chances, but use his ignorance to shelve him in Elf Hill for the next century or two.

But why hadn't they just slipped a knife in his ribs? That should have been easy enough to do. Indeed, the attack of the hollow knight must have been such an attempt. When that failed, Alfric had changed tactics and used guile. How had the Duke known about him in the first place? Mother Gerd, of course. The demon she raised must have told her something about Holger which made her direct him to her powerful acquaintance in Faerie. No doubt she sent the news of him ahead by magical means. She must have hoped Alfric could take care of him.

But what had the demon said? And, murder and trickery having failed, what would the Middle World try next?

Anyhow, this avenue of return to his world was closed. He'd have to cast around for another way. Judging from what he had seen and heard, there were white magicians as well as black. Maybe he could consult one of them. He had no intention of mixing into the struggle here if he could avoid it. One war at a time, please! Alfric would have done best to act honestly and send him home as he asked.

Which consideration fairly well proved Alfric was unable to.

Something laughed in the fog, low and hideously. Holger started. Hugi clapped his hands to his ears. They heard leather wings pass overhead. Still all they could see was the dripping grayness.

"The thing seems to be in front of us," muttered Holger. "If we turn aside——"

"Nay." Alianora's lips trembled, but she spoke gamely. " 'Tis a trick to get us off the path. Once lost in these clouds, we're indeed without hope."

"Okay," said Holger out of a sandy throat. "I'll go first."

That was a nerve-racking ride, where shapes went slipping and sliding on the fringe of sight, where the air was evil with slitherings and hissings, howls and laughs. Once a blind horrible face appeared before him. It hung in the vapor and mouthed. He plowed stubbornly ahead and it receded before him. Hugi shut his eyes and chanted, "I ha' been a guid dwarf. I ha' been a guid dwarf. I ha' been a guid dwarf."

It seemed forever before the mist lifted. That was on the border of the dusk land. Papillon and the unicorn were first to scent the sun. They broke into gallop, burst out and neighed at the light.

The time was nearing evening. They had emerged at a different point from where they entered. Long shadows of crags and conifers fell across hills rough with gorse. The wind slid thin and cold around Holger; he heard the boom of a waterfall. Nonetheless, after—how many days?—in Faerie, the natural world was a sight to catch at a man's heart.

"Yon Pharisees can pursue us after dark," said Alianora. "Yet their spells be less strong out here, so we've better hope." Her tone was dull with weariness. Holger began to feel how tired he was too.

They urged their mounts forward, to get as far as possible before sundown. When they made camp, it was high on a slope overgrown with pines. Holger lopped two saplings with his sword and made a cross of them, which he planted near the bonfire they'd keep going all night. Hugi's precautions were more pagan, a ring of stones and iron objects laid down with incantations.

"Now," said Alianora, "methinks we'll last the dark hours." She smiled at Holger. "I've not yet told ye how valiantly ye fought, back there at the castle. Ho, 'twas a bra sight!"

"Why, uh, uh, thanks." Holger looked at his feet, which dug at the ground. He didn't really mind being admired by a pretty girl, but—he wasn't sure what. To cover his confusion, he sat down and examined the dagger he had won from Alfric. A bone handle and a disproportionately large basket hilt were fixed to a thin blade which he decided must be magnesium. The pure metal was too soft to make a very good weapon, not to mention being inflammable; but since Alfric had evidently set store by the knife, Holger would keep it. He rummaged in his saddlebags and, besides some homely equipment like a jar of oil, turned up an extra misericord. Hugi could wear that unsheathed. Holger scabbarded the magnesium blade to his belt near his steel knife. By then, Alianora had prepared dinner from what supplies remained.

Night stole over them. Holger, who would take the third watch, lay his length on the soft needles of the forest floor. The fire burned warm and red. One by one his nerves eased. To be sure, he couldn't fall asleep. Not under these circumstances. Too bad. He needed his sleep. . . .

He woke with a jerk. Alianora was shaking him. In the restless light he saw her eyes grown enormous. Her voice was a dry whisper. "List! There's summat out there!"

He got up, sword in hand, and peered into the gloom. Yes, he could hear them too, the *pad-pad-pad* of many feet, and he saw the light gleam off slanted eyes.

A wolf howled, almost in his ear. He leaped and slashed with his sword. Laughter answered, shrill and nasty. *"In nomine Patris,"* he called, and was mocked by the noises. Either those things were immune to holy names, or they weren't close enough to be hurt. Probably the former. As his eyes adapted, he saw the shadows. They glided around and around the charmed circle. They were monstrous.

Hugi crouched by the fire; his teeth clapped in his head. Alianora moaned and crept into Holger's free arm. He felt how she shuddered. "Take it easy," he said.

"But the sendings," she gasped. "Night-gangers on every hand, Holger! I've never erenow been under their siege. I canna look." She buried her face against his shoulder. Her fingers tightened on his arm till the nails bit.

"This is new to me also," he said. Funny how unfrightened he was. The prowlers were horrible to see, of course, but why watch them? Especially when he had Alianora to watch instead. Thank God for a phlegmatic temperament! "They can't get at us, dear," he said. "If they could, they would. Therefore they can't."

"But—but——"

"I've seen dammed rivers that could drown a whole valley. No one worried. They knew the dam would hold."

Privately, he wondered what the safety factor of the camp's charms was. No doubt magicians in this world had their equivalent of the Rubber Handbook, with tables of such data. Or if not, they jolly well ought to. He had to go by God and by guess, but somehow—another buried memory?—he felt their defenses were strong enough.

"Just take it easy," he said. "We'll be all right. They can't do more than keep us awake with that infernal racket."

She was still atremble, so he kissed her. She responded with an uncertain, inexperienced clumsiness. He grinned out at the hosts of the Middle World. If they were going to sit and watch him neck, he hoped they'd learn something.

10

BEFORE DAWN THE ENEMY departed. Hugi said they must get back to their lairs in plenty of time. Holger wondered what they couldn't stand about sunlight. Actinic radiation? If so, he wished he had an ultraviolet lamp.

Hoy, wait! That explained Alfric's magnesium dagger. The thing was only incidentally a stabbing weapon. If hard pressed by his Middle World rivals, the Duke could ignite the metal. The hilt would shade his hand from the intense ultraviolet emission; no doubt he'd pull a cloak over his face with the other hand. His opponents would have to flee. Well, such an emergency aid was nice for a mortal man too.

Having slept fitfully, Holger, Hugi, and Alianora caught a two or three hours' nap before breakfast. When the Dane awoke, he found himself naked. His Faerie garments had vanished. That was rather petty of Alfric, he thought. Luckily, Alianora was still asleep: not that he supposed she would have been embarrassed, but he would. He scrambled into his old traveling clothes, including hauberk and helmet.

More refreshed than he had expected, they prepared to ride on. Alianora still had the unicorn; he wondered what her influence over the shy beast was. "Now where should we go?" he asked.

"I dinna know for certain," she replied, "save that we'd best seek dwellings o' men. 'Tis clear that Faerie is out after ye, Holger"—she used the intimate pronoun now, and smiled adoringly at him—"but the soulless ones canna go nigh a kirk, so we can at least gain a respite. Afterward, though, we must seek a shielding o' powerful magic, white magic."

"Where?"

"I ken one warlock, in Tarnberg village, with a good heart and some skill. Thither should we wend, methinks."

"Okay. But what if this local marvel finds he can't bat against the big-league pitchers?" Holger saw bewilderment begin to mar her worshipful gaze and hastily explained, "I mean, supposing a country practitioner like that can't match himself with such experts as Alfric and Morgan le Fay?"

"Then belike ye should seek the Empire. 'Tis far to the west, a hard perilous journey, but they'd welcome a strong knicht." She sighed, misty-eyed. "And no since Carl's day has there been one like ye."

"Who was this Carl?" he asked. "I've heard the name before."

"Why, the founder o' the Holy Empire. The king who made Christendie strong and rolled the Saracens back into Spain. Carl the Great, Carolus Magnus, surely ye've heard o' him."

"Mmmm . . . maybe I have." Holger searched his mind. It was hard to tell what part of his knowledge came from his education and what from those inexplicable memories that were rising even more often within him. "Do you mean Charlemagne?"

"So some call him. I see his fame has reached even to your South Carolina. 'Tis said he had many bold knights to serve him, though I've only heard tales o' that Roland who fell at Roncesvalles."

Holger's brain went into a spin. Was he really in the past? No, impossible. And yet Charlemagne was certainly a historical figure.

Ah, he had it. The Carolingian cycle, the *Chansons de Geste*, the later medieval prose romances and folk ballads. Yes, that fitted. Fairyland and Saracens, swan-mays and unicorns, witchcraft and Elf Hill, Roland and Oliver— Holy jumping Judas! Had he somehow fallen into a . . . a book?

No, that didn't make sense. It was much the most reasonable to keep on supposing this was another universe, a complete space-time continuum with its own laws of nature. Given a large enough number of such universes, one of them was bound to fit any arbitrary pattern, such as that of pre-Renaissance European legendry.

Though matters couldn't be quite that simple. His irruption had not been into any random cosmos, for no reason whatsoever; too many elements of his experiences were too appropriate to something or other. So: between his home world and this, some connection existed. Not only the astronomy and geography showed parallels, the very details of history did. The Carl of this world could not be identical with the Charlemagne of his, but somehow they had fulfilled corresponding roles. The mystics, dreamers, poets, and hack writers of home had in some unconscious way been in tune with whatever force linked the two universes; the corpus of stories which they gradually evolved had been a better job of reporting than they knew.

Doubtless more than two continua were involved. Perhaps all were. All the uncounted stellar universes might be separate facets of one transcendental existence. Holger didn't pursue that idea. He had more immediate questions. What else could he identify in this world?

Well, Hugi had spoken of Morgan as King Arthur's sister. *The* Arthur! Holger wished he had read the old tales more closely; he had only a dim childhood recollection of them.

As for the rest, let's see, Carl's paladins had included Roland and Oliver and Huon and—whoa. Where did he remember Huon from? The dark strange face rose in his mind, the sardonic humor which had so often irritated the others: Huon de Bordeaux, yes, he had finally gone off and become a king or duke or something in Faerie. *But how do I know that?*

Hugi's grumble broke his train of thought. Half-grasped memories scurried back down into hiding. " 'Twill na be a funnish trip, this, if each nicht we maun list to they long-legged beasties howl beyond the firelicht."

"Nay, I think no they'll keep that up," answered Alianora. " 'Tis o' no use to them, sairly now when they must be busied gathering their hosts for war." She frowned. "Yet belike they'll try summat else. Alfric's no one to surrender a prey."

That idea was scarcely pleasant company.

They scrambled higher into the hills, bearing northwest at the girl's direction. By noon they were far up. Here the land was cliffs and crags and boulders, wiry grass, an occasional tree twisted and stunted. They could see widely on each side, from the receding darkness of Faerie to the stark heights they must cross, and straight down into canyons which rang with the noise of glacial rivers. The sky was pale, ragged streamers of cloud hurrying across it, the light chill and brilliant.

They took shelter behind a bluff when they stopped for lunch. Holger, gnawing away at a slab of stone-hard bread and a hunk of rubbery cheese, could not resist griping. "Is Denmark the only land in creation where they know how to make a decent sandwich? Now if you gave me some thin-sliced pumpernickel, baby shrimp, eggs and——"

"Ye cook too?" Alianora looked at him with awe.

"Uh, not exactly, but——"

She snuggled close against him. He found that a bit disconcerting, having grown up with the idea . . . or illusion . . . that the man takes the initiative. "Come the chance," she murmured, "I shall fetch what ye require, and we shall ha' us a feast, the two o' us alone."

"Hm," said Hugi. "Methinks I'll go squint at the weather."

"Hey, come back!" yelped Holger, but the dwarf had already gone around the bluff.

"He's a good little man," said Alianora. She laid her arms around Holger's neck. "He kens when a lass needs comforting."

"Now, wait a minute. Look here, I mean, you're awfully nice and I like you a lot. But. I mean—— Oh, hell. Never mind." Holger gathered her in.

Hugi landed almost in their laps. "A dragon!" he screamed. "A dragon flying hither!"

"Huh?" Holger jumped up, spilling Alianora. "What? Where?"

"A firedrake, och, och, 'tis been sent by Alfric and noo we're done!" Hugi clung to the man's knees. "Save us, Sir Knicht! Is 't no yer business to slay dragons?"

Papillon snorted and shivered. The unicorn was already off. Alianora ran after it, whistling. It stopped long enough for her to spring on its back, and then leaped from sight. Holger snatched Hugi, mounted, and galloped on her trail.

As he topped the bluff, he could see the monster. It came from the south, still half a mile away, but already the thunderclap wingbeats hit his ears. Fifty feet long, he thought in a vortex of panic. Fifty feet of scale-armored muscle, a snake head which could swallow him in two bites, bat wings and iron talons. He didn't need to spur Papillon. The horse was crazed with fear, running almost as fast as the unicorn. Sparks flew from his shod hoofs. The noise of them on rock was lost in the nearing roar of dragon wings.

"Yi-yi-yi!" wailed Hugi. " 'Tis roasted we'll be!"

Downward the monster slanted, overhauling them with nightmare speed. Holger glanced back again and saw flame and smoke roll from the fanged mouth. For a lunatic moment he wondered about the metabolism; and what amendment to the square-cube law permitted that hulk to fly? A whiff of sulfur dioxide stabbed his nostrils.

"Look yonder!" Alianora's cry drifted down the slope. He gazed the way she pointed and saw a narrow cave mouth in a nearby cliff. "He canna follow us in there!"

"No!" bellowed Holger. "Keep out of that! It's death!"

She cast him a frightened glance, but obediently urged the unicorn away from the cave. Holger felt the first billow of heat on his back. Ye gods, if they went to earth in that hole, the dragon could suffocate them with six puffs.

"We've got to find water!" he bawled.

Up and over the stony land they fled, while the thresh of wings and the rumble of flames grew louder. Holger drew his sword. But what chance would he have? The dragon could grill him in his hauberk.

Well, he thought, *I may win a chance for Alianora to get clear.*

He didn't stop to reason out why he must find water. There was only time to flee, over the hills, along a precipice edge, down a gorge. Papillon screamed as fire touched him.

Then they burst through a screen of brush, and a river ran below them, green and swift and thirty feet wide. The unicorn plunged in. Spray sheeted about the spiral horn. Papillon followed. They stopped in midstream. The river was icy cold, daggers in their feet.

The dragon landed on the bank. It arched its back and hissed like an angry locomotive. Afraid of water, Holger realized. So that was what his intuition had known.

" 'Twill fly above, snatch us into the air," gasped Alianora.

"Get down, then!" Holger leaped to the pebbly streambed. The current swirled strong around his chest. Hugi and Alianora clung to the tails of their respective mounts. "When the attack comes, duck below the surface," Holger commanded.

But no human could stay down long enough. They were done.

Yeah, done to a turn.

The dragon flapped clumsily aloft. Its shadow fell on them as it hovered against the sun. Slowly, it descended. Flame gushed ahead, out of the open jaws.

Flame! Holger sheathed his sword, snatched off his helmet, and scooped it full of water. The dragon rushed down. He threw up one arm to protect his eyes. Blindly, he sloshed.

Steam burst around him. The dragon bellowed, nearly splitting his eardrums. The scaled bulk wobbled in flight, long neck dashing to and fro, tail churning the stream. Holger cursed and threw another helmetful of water at its snout.

The dragon stunned him with a shriek. Slowly and painfully, it rose in the air and flew back south. They heard its clamor for a long while.

The breath sobbed into Holger's lungs. He stood motionless, exhausted, till the beast was out of sight. Finally he led the others back to shore.

"Holger, Holger!" Alianora clung to him, trembled and wept and laughed.

"How'd ye do it? How'd ye conquer him, best o' knichts, darling, my jo?"

"Oh, well. That." Holger felt his face gingerly. He'd gotten several blisters. "A little thermodynamics is all."

"What manner o' magic be that?" she asked with reverence.

"Not magic. Look, if the creature breathed fire, then it had to be even hotter inside. So I tossed half a gallon of water down its gullet. Caused a small boiler explosion." Holger waved his hand with elaborate casualness. "Nothing to it."

11

A FEW MILES farther on they entered a hollow sheltered by cliff walls, as mild and sunny as any lowland. Beech and poplar rustled above long grass full of primroses, a brook tinkled, a flock of starlings fluttered off. The place seemed ideal for a rest such as they and the mounts badly needed.

After a defensive circle was constructed, Alianora yawned—she could do even that quite charmingly—and curled up to sleep. Hugi sat down below the cross, whittling with his new knife. Holger felt restless. "I think I'll take a look around," he said. "Call me if anything goes wrong."

"Is 't safe to gang off alane?" said the dwarf. He answered himself: "Aye, o' coorse 'tis. What can harm a drakeslayer?"

Holger blushed. He was the man of the hour, but knew much too well what a series of accidents had caused that. "I won't go far."

He got his pipe lighted and strolled off, jingling a bit. The scene was utterly peaceful: meadow, flowers, trees, water, Papillon and the unicorn cropping, the liquid notes of a thrush. Except for the smart of his burns, he could easily have sat down, blotted up sunshine, and considered Alianora. But no. He wrenched his mind away. He had some heavier thinking to do.

Let's admit it, he was a crucial figure, or at least an important one, in this Carolingian world. In view of everything that had happened, it must be more than coincidence that Papillon, preternaturally strong and intelligent, should have been waiting exactly where he appeared, with clothes and arms that exactly fitted his own outsize frame. Then there was the excitement he had caused in Faerie, and the curious fact that despite his ignorance they had not been able to kill him. . . . Well, there had been a Charlemagne in both worlds. Maybe he himself was also, somehow, doubled. But then who was he? And why, and how?

He lost sight of the camp as he wandered on, trying to fit what he had learned into a pattern. This business of Chaos versus Law, for example, turned out to be more than religious dogma. It was a practical fact of existence, here. He was reminded of the second law of thermodynamics, the tendency of the physical universe toward disorder and level entropy. Perhaps here, that tendency found a more . . . animistic . . . expression. Or, wait a minute, didn't it in his own world too? What had he been fighting when he fought the Nazis but a resurgence of archaic horrors that civilized men had once believed were safely dead?

In this universe the wild folk of the Middle World might be trying to break down a corresponding painfully established order: to restore some primeval state where anything could happen. Decent humanity would, on the other hand, always want to strengthen and extend Law, safety, predictability. Therefore Christianity, Judaism, even Mohammedanism frowned on witchcraft, that was more allied to Chaos than to orderly physical nature. Though to be sure, science had its perversions, while magic had its laws. A definite ritual was needed in either case, whether you built an airplane or a flying carpet. Gerd had mentioned something about the impersonal character of the supernatural. Yes, that was why Roland had tried to break Durindal, in his last hour at Roncesvalles: so the miraculous sword would not fall into paynim hands. . . .

The symmetry was suggestive. In Holger's home world, physical forces were strong and well understood, mental-magical forces weak and unmanageable. In this universe the opposite held true. Both worlds were, in some obscure way, one; the endless struggle between Law and Chaos had reached a simultaneous climax in them. As for the force which made them so parallel, the ultimate oneness itself, he supposed he would have to break down and call it God. But he lacked a theological bent of mind. He'd rather stick to what he had directly observed, and to immediate practical problems. Such as his own reason for being here.

But that continued to elude him. He remembered a life in the other world, from childhood to a certain moment on the beach near Kronborg. Somehow he had had another life too, but he didn't know where or when. Those memories had been stolen. No, rather, they had been forced back into his subconscious, and only under unusual stimuli did they return.

A thought drifted through him. *Cortana.* Where had he heard that name? Oh, yes, the nickel had mentioned it. Cortana was a sword. It had been full of magic, but now lay buried away from sight of man. *Once I held Cortana when brands were flashing on a stricken field.*

He walked around a clump of trees. Morgan le Fay stood waiting.

At first he couldn't move. His heart hammered; a curious darkness passed over him, and the darkness was beautiful. She came forward, tinged by the gold light that filtered down through green leaves. Her dress was like snow, her lips a coral curve, her hair shining as a starlit deep lake. All he could see to begin with were the colors. Her tone flowed into him.

"Greeting, Holger. How long it has been!"

He fought for calmness, and lost. Morgan took his hands. She was tall, her smile didn't have far to go before it rocked him. "And how lonely I have been for you," she murmured.

"For *me?*" His voice broke in an idiotic squeak.

"Aye, who else? Have you forgotten that too?" She called him "thou," making the word a caress. "Indeed a night was laid on you. You have been long away, Holger."

"Bu-bu-bu-but——"

She laughed, not as ordinary humans do but as if laughter itself laughed most softly. "Ah, your poor face! Few men could have stood up to the firedrake as you did. Let me heal those burns." Her fingers touched them. He felt pain and blisters vanish. "There, now, are you more comfortable?"

As a matter of fact, he wasn't. He was perspiring, and the cloak seemed too tight around his neck. Enough wit had returned for him to notice details, but they weren't the sort to calm a man: pale perfect features, feline grace of movement, a body with more curves than a scenic highway.

"You've gotten some uncouth habits in the other world." She took the pipe from his slack mouth, shook it out, and stuck it into the pouch at his belt. On the way back her hand slipped along his side and came to rest on his upper arm. "Naughty boy!"

That gave him back a measure of self-possession. Big women had no business acting kittenish. Nor was that any way to treat a pipe. "Look here," he croaked. "You were with Alfric, and he's been doing his best to kill me. What do you want with me?"

"What does any woman want, who longs for a man?" She sidled closer. Holger backed up till a tree stopped him.

"In truth," said Morgan, "I knew not who you were, and aided Alfric unwittingly. The instant I learned of his deception, I hastened to find you."

He wiped the sweat off his brow. "That's a lie," he said harshly.

"Well, we of the gentler sex must be permitted a little fancifulness, must we not, my sweet?" She patted his cheek. "It's God's truth that I have come to win you back."

"Win me back to Chaos!" he blustered.

"And why not? What is there about dull Law that drives you to defend it? See, I am honest with you; now do you be honest with yourself. Why, Holger, my darling bear, you're but bulwarking loutish peasants and fat-gutted burghers, when the mirth and thunder and blazing stars of Chaos could be yours. When were you ever one for a safe and narrow life, locked in its own smugness, roofed with a sour gray sky, stinking of smoke and dung—you who drove armies from the field? You could hurl suns and shape worlds if you chose!"

Her head lay on his breast and her arms about his waist. "N-n-no!" he stuttered. "I don't trust——"

"Ah, lackaday! Is this the man who dwelt so long with me in Avalon? Have you forgotten what centuries I gave you of youth, and lordship, and love?" She looked up at him again with huge dark eyes. He told himself how corny her act was, but didn't believe his own claim. "If you will not join with us, then at least do not fight against us. Return to Avalon, Holger. Come back with me to Avalon the fair."

Somewhere in his buckling mind he knew that for a change she was sincere. She wanted him out from underfoot in the coming battle, but she also wanted him, period. *And why not?* his thought lurched. What did he owe to either side, in this universe that was not his? When Morgan le Fay embraced him——

"Such long years," she whispered, "and when we meet you have not even kissed me."

"That," he choked, "c-c-could be remedied."

It was rather like being in a soft cyclone. He couldn't concentrate on anything else. Not that he wanted to.

"Ah-h-h," she breathed at last, her eyes still closed, "my lord, my lord, kiss me again. Kiss me forever."

He collected her. A flicker of white caught the corner of his eye. He raised his head and saw Alianora on the unicorn. She was just rounding the nearby thicket. "Holger," she called, "Holger, dear, where be ye—oh!"

The unicorn reared and threw her to the grass. With a thunderous indignant snort, the animal fled. Alianora sprang up and glared at Holger and Morgan. "Now see wha' ye ha' done!" she wailed irrationally. "He'll ne'er come back!"

Holger disentangled himself. Alianora burst into tears.

"Get that peasant wench out of here!" cried Morgan in a fury.

Alianora flared up. "Get away yourself!" she screeched. "Foul witch that ye be, get away from him!"

The queen's teeth gleamed forth. "Holger, if that beanpole betake herself not hence this very minute——"

"Beanpole!" yelled Alianora. "Why, ye overstuffed fleshpot. I'll claw your popeyes out!"

"Little girls shouldn't cry," snarled Morgan. "They'll grow up even homelier than they are."

Alianora clenched her fists and stalked closer. "Better a wee bit young than ha' my skin sag wi' eld."

"You have such pretty skin," hissed Morgan. "How did you ever achieve that peeling-sunburn effect?"

"Not in the shop where ye bought your complexion," said Alianora.

Holger crept aside, wondering how to get out of this alive.

"I see you're a swan-may," said Morgan. "Have you laid any good eggs lately?"

"Nay. I canna cackle so shrill as some old hens."

Morgan flushed and raised her hands in a violent pass. "See how you like being a hen yourself!"

"Hey!" Holger leaped forward. He didn't intend to strike her, but one arm encountered Morgan and the queen went rolling over in the grass.

"None of that," he gasped.

She got slowly to her feet. Color and expression had alike departed her countenance. "So that is how it stands," she said.

"I guess it is," said Holger, and wondered if he meant it.

"Well, have your way, then. We'll meet again, my friend." Morgan laughed, an ugly sound this time, and waved. Suddenly she was gone. There was a bang as air rushed in where she had stood.

Alianora began to cry in earnest. She leaned against a tree bole and buried her face in one arm. When Holger went to lay a hand on her shoulder, she shook him off. "Go away," she mumbled. "G-g-g-o off wi' your witch, sith she p-p-please ye so well. Uh-h-h——"

"It wasn't my fault," said Holger helplessly. "I didn't ask her to come."

"I willna hearken, I tell ye. Go away."

Holger decided he had troubles enough without a hysterical female on his hands. He pulled her around, shook her, and said between his teeth, "I have nothing to do with this. Hear? Now will you come along like a grown human being, or must I drag you?"

Alianora gulped, stared at him with wide wet eyes, and dropped her lashes. He noticed how long they were. "I'll come wi' ye," she said meekly.

Holger got his pipe going again and fumed most of the way back. Damn, damn, damn, and damn! Almost, there with Morgan le Fay, he had remembered that other life. Almost, and now the knowledge was gone again.

Well, too late. From this day on she'd doubtless be his bitterest opponent. Though in all frankness it was probably a good thing that they'd been interrupted. He couldn't have held out against her blandishments much longer.

And the worst part was, he rather wished he hadn't. Who had written that line about nothing being so futile as the memory of a temptation resisted?

Too late. He'd just have to carry on.

His buried self shot a gleam into his conscious mind, and he knew why the unicorn had departed. Morgan le Fay must have been the last straw on its outraged sensibilities—or the last dozen straws. That made him chuckle, and he took Alianora's hand. They walked back to camp side by side.

12

THEY WERE NOT PLAGUED that night, which Hugi said was without a doubt because something worse was being prepared. Holger was inclined to share the dwarf's pessimism. And now they had only one mount, for three people. Of course Alianora could spend some of her travel time aloft; but swans aren't hovering birds, and they dared not let her get too far ahead. However great his endurance, Papillon couldn't carry a large warrior in chain mail, a girl, a half-pint man, and their gear, at anything like his normal speed.

So they made an early start, and Alianora in swan shape studied their best route from above. She came back to sit behind the saddle, arms around Holger's waist (which compensated for a lot of nuisances), and guided him. By dusk she hoped they could reach the pass and tomorrow the edge of human habitation. There were still many miles of wilderness to travel on the other side of the range, but she had seen a few clearings, isolated farmsteads and hamlets. "And where'er several men dwell, if they be not evil doers, will belike lie hallowed ground—a shrine, if naught else—which most o' the creatures that dog us dare no approach closely."

"But in that case," Holger asked, "how can the Middle World even think of seizing human land?"

"By help o' beings who need no fear daylicht or priestcraft. Animals like yon dragon; creatures wi' souls, like bad dwarfs. However, such allies be too few, and mostly too stupid, to have more than special use. Chiefly, methinks, the Middle World will depend on humans who'll fight for Chaos. Witches, warlocks, bandits, murderers, 'fore all the heathen savages o' the north and south. These can desecrate the sacred places and slay such men as battle against them. Then the rest o' the humans will flee, and there'll be naught left to prevent the blue gloaming being drawn over hundreds o' leagues more. With every such advance, the realms of Law will grow weaker: not alone in numbers, but in spirit, for the near presence o' Chaos must affect the good folk, turning them skittish, lawless, and inclined to devilments o' their own." Alianora shook her head, troubled. "As evil waxes, the very men who stand for good will in their fear use ever worse means o' fighting, and thereby give evil a free beach-head."

Holger thought of his own world, where Coventry had been avenged upon Cologne, and nodded. His helmet felt suddenly heavy.

As much to escape that remembrance as for any other reason, he turned back to immediate things. The powers of his persecutors were not unlimited, or he would have been stopped long ago. What were the limits, then? Curiously, for beings said to be soulless, the Faerie race were under severe physical handicaps, and must rely mainly on guile. Except for being fast and supple, none of them were anywhere near a match for a normally strong man. (To be sure, giants, trolls, and various other Middle World beings did have more brute power than humans, but Alianora said they were slow and clumsy.) None could endure the sun; hence their excursions into the human domain could only take place after dark. Even at such times they must avoid sacred objects. Their spells would bounce like billiard balls off anyone in a state of grace; simply the usual modicum of decency and determination would get a man through. You could be killed by them, or through their machinations; you could be fooled, dazzled, victimized; but in a certain ultimate sense, you could not be conquered unless you wanted to be.

Also, the force of a spell seemed to depend on distance. The farther he got from Faerie, the safer Holger would probably be from its inhabitants.

Not that Alfric could be laughed off. On the contrary. He was not the head of the enemy. Morgan le Fay outranked him, and beyond her must be others, clear on to a final One whom Holger did not wish to think about. But Alfric had many powers, he was wily and skillful, and he had not given up. Morgan had hardly begun yet.

If I only knew what they want me for.

That whole day the horse climbed. As the sun went down, Holger drew rein atop the pass. Grass grew in sparse clumps among strewn rocks, otherwise the place was bare. A bleak wind ran up the cliffs and over the ridge. Papillon blew out his lips in a sigh. His head drooped.

"Poor beastie." Alianora stroked the velvet muzzle. "We've used ye hard, have we no? And naught better tonicht than a few dry weeds." She found a rock with a depression on top and poured patiently from a waterskin till he had drunk enough. Holger rubbed down the stallion himself. He had begun to take his cavalier's skills for granted, but was rather surprised at the overflow of his affection for this Papillon. He arranged the sadly torn and muddy silk trappings into a sort of coat for the horse. With camp established, supper bolted, and themselves worn out, the travelers retired.

Alianora stood the first watch, then Holger, finally Hugi. When he had composed himself beside the girl, Holger found he couldn't get back to sleep. Somehow her head had gotten pillowed on his shoulder and one arm thrown across his chest. He couldn't hear her breathing above the wind, but he felt the slight steady movement; felt too how she seemed to radiate heat where she touched him. Elsewhere he was damnably cold, the chill seeped through the cloaks which covered them. The saddle blanket beneath did little to take the curse off the hard ground.

But that wasn't why he stayed wakeful. When danger had sharpened all his senses, and then this creature of warmth and tousled hair lay practically on top of him . . . He tried to pass the time with recollections of Meriven, but that only made matters worse. And at this moment, he thought bitterly, he could have been with Morgan le Fay.

Leaving Alianora alone, when the enemy marched? No! Almost unconsciously, he reached for her. That was another mistake. Before he quite knew what had happened, his hand had slipped beneath her feather tunic and cupped a soft young breast. She stirred, murmuring in her sleep. He didn't move again, but neither had he the strength to withdraw his hand. Finally, shaken, his skin prickling, he opened his eyes.

The stars glittered like winter. There was no moon, but from the position of Carl's Wain (even in heaven they remember you, my King!) he judged sunrise was not far off. The blackness on earth was nearly absolute. He saw Hugi's outline hunched by the low red fire, otherwise only an upthrust of masses against the sky. That crag yonder—

He'd never seen that crag before!

Holger sprang to his feet a moment ahead of the earth shock. It came again, and yet again, a sound like monstrous drums; the mountain shook as a house shakes when a heavy man climbs the stairs. Holger heard stones go bounding and shattering down the slope. He snatched his sword, and then the giant was upon them.

A foot as long as Holger himself kicked the guardian ring aside. The firelight limned great unclipped toenails. Alianora cried out. Holger shoved her behind him. Papillon sprang toward the man, a neigh of defiance, neck and tail arched, nostrils dilated. Hugi scuttled to join Alianora.

The giant squatted down and poked up the fire with a forefinger like a shaggy staff. As flames guttered high, Holger saw the creature was humanoid, though grotesquely squat and short-legged in proportion to height. *Well*, his thought flashed, *even if the law of proportion doesn't work quite the same here as at home, he needs enough cross section to bear his weight.* The uncouth body wore skins, crudely stitched together; what whiff he caught made Holger glad he was upwind. As nearly as could be judged in that tangled hair and beard, the giant's features were acromegalic, eyes roofed with bony ridges, nose and jaw jutting coarsely forth, heavy lips and grisly huge teeth.

"Get on Papillon, Hugi," said Holger. Now that the first shock was past, he stopped being afraid. He didn't dare be. "I'll hold him as long as I can. Alianora, you get airborne."

"I'll stand wi' ye." Her voice was small, but she trod up beside him with chin lifted.

"Hoo could it ha' happened?" moaned Hugi. "He's o' Middle World breed. The charms would balk him."

"He stalked us," said Alianora roughly. "Such folk can gang quiet when they will. He waited for a moment when there was such ungodliness o' thocht in our midst that the holy signs were annulled." Her glance accused the cowering dwarf. Holger knew with wretchedness that Hugi was not to blame. But——

"Talk so I can hear you!"

That giant did not speak deafeningly loud, nor was his accent too barbarous. What made him hard to understand was the pitch: so low that the inaudible bottom registers shivered in human bones. Holger wet his lips, stepped forward, and said in his own deepest voice, "In the name of the Father, and the Son, and the Holy Ghost, I bid you begone."

"Haw!" fleered the giant. "Too late for that, mortal, when you've broken the good circle by your sinful wishes and not yet made act of contrition." He reached out a hand. "Alfric told me I'd find tender prey on this path. Give me the maiden, and you may continue."

Holger wanted to throw back some ringing challenge, suitable to his disgust at any such notion. By God, there were worse things than death! Unfortunately, he could only think of a phrase unfit for the maiden's ears. He lunged instead. His sword blazed across the immense knuckles.

The giant yanked his hand back, blew on the smoking wound, and cried: "Hold! Let's talk!" Nearly blasted off his feet by the volume, Holger paused.

To him, who was used to being the largest person around, the face above his seemed even broader than it was. But he stood fast and heard the basso profundissimo say in a rather reasonable tone:

"Look here, mortal, I sense you're a great champion. And of course the touch of iron hurts me. Yet there's a lot of me, and I could belike crush you with stones before you got in too many blows. What say we contest an easier way? If you win by your wit, you may go on unmolested. In fact, I'll give you a helmetful of gold." He pointed to a wallet at his side which must hold a hundredweight or more. "If you lose, you surrender the girl to me."

"No!" Holger spat on the earth.

"Wait. Wait, darling." Alianora seized his arm with sudden eagerness. "Ask him if he means a riddling contest."

Puzzled, Holger did. The giant nodded. "Aye. For know, we of the Great Folk sit in our halls throughout the endless winter night of our homeland, year after year, century after century, and pass the time with contests of skill. Above all are we fond of riddles. It were worth my while to let you pass, could you give me three new ones of which I cannot answer two, that I may use them in turn." His bestial visage turned eastward, anxiously. "Be quick, though."

Alianora's eyes kindled. "I thocht so, Holger. Make the bargain. Ye can outtrick him." The giant showed no comprehension. Of course, Holger realized. A creature that big couldn't hear far into the human range of frequencies.

He answered falsetto, "I can't think of anything."

"Ye can." Her confidence sank a little. She stared at the ground and dug with one toe. "If ye canna, well, let him have me. He only wants me to eat. Ye mean too much, Holger, to the whole world, methinks, to risk death in a fight over nobbut me."

He groped in his bewilderment. What puzzles did he know? "Four hanging, four ganging, two leading, one trailing: a cow." Samson's poser to the Philistines. A few such. But surely over the centuries, the ogre had heard them. And he, Holger, wasn't bright enough to invent a brain teaser on such short notice.

"I'd rather fight for someone I know, like you, than——" he began. The squatting monster interrupted him with a gruff "Hurry, I say!"

A wild idea coursed through Holger. "Can't he stand the sun?" he asked Alianora in his stage-eunuch tone.

"Nay," she said. "The bricht rays turn his flesh to stone."

"Oh-ho," squeaked Hugi, "if ye hold his mind fast eneugh, lad, so dawn comes on him unawares, then we can loot yon bag o' gold."

"I dinna know about that," said Alianora. "I've heard treasure won by such a trick is cursed, and the man who wins it soon dies. But Holger, in an hour he must flee the dawn. Can ye no delay him an hour, ye who overcame the dragon?"

"I . . . think . . . so." Holger swung back on the colossus, who was beginning to growl in angry impatience. "I'll contest with you," he said.

"For this one night, then," said the giant. His grin was sadistic. "Perhaps another night after that . . . Well, bind the wench so she can't flee. Hurry!"

Holger moved as slowly as he dared. Tying Alianora's wrists, he piped, "You can throw off this knot, if worst comes to worst."

"Nay, I willna flee, or he'll turn on ye."

"He'll have to fight me anyway," said Holger. "You might as well save your own life." But he couldn't sound very heroic in falsetto.

He threw some more sticks on the fire and turned to the giant, who had sat down with knees under hairy chin. "Here we go," he said.

"Good. You will be glad to know for your honor, I am the riddle champion of nine flintgarths." The giant looked at Alianora and smacked his lips. "A delicate morsel."

Holger's sword was aloft before he knew what he was about. "Hold your foul tongue!" he roared.

"Would you liefer fight?" The vast muscles bunched.

"No." Holger checked his temper. But that such a hippo dared look on his Alianora——! "Okay," he snapped. "First riddle. Why does a chicken cross the road?"

"What?" The giant gaped till his teeth shone like wet rocks. "You ask me that?"

"I do."

"But the veriest child knows. To get to the other side."

Holger shook his yellow-maned head. "Wrong."

"You lie!" The mammoth shape half rose.

Holger swung his sword whistling. "I have a perfectly good answer," he said. "You must find it."

"I never heard the like," complained the giant. But he seated himself and tugged his beard with one filthy hand. "Why does a chicken cross the road? Why not, if not to get to the other side? What mystical intent is here? What might a chicken and a road represent?" He shut his eyes and swayed back and forth. Alianora, lying bound near the fire, gave Holger a cheer.

After an endlessness of cold wind and colder stars, Holger saw the eyes of the monster open. They glowed in the firelight like two blood-colored lamps, deep under the cavernous brows. "I have the answer," said the terrifying voice. " 'Tis not unlike the one that Thiazi baffled Grotnir with, five hundred winters agone. See you, mortal, a chicken is the human soul, and the road is life which must be crossed, from the ditch of birth to the ditch of death. On that road are many perils, not alone the ruts of toil and the mire of sin, but wagons of war and pestilence, drawn by the oxen of destruction; while overhead wheels that hawk hight Satan, ever ready to stoop. The chicken knows not why it crosses the road, save that it sees greener fields on the far side. It crosses because it must, even as we all must."

He beamed smugly. Holger shook his head. "No, wrong again."

"*What?* Why, you——" The ogre surged erect.

"So you'd rather fight?" said Holger. "I knew you had no intellectual staying power."

"No, no, no!" howled the giant, starting a minor landslide. He stalked about for a while before getting enough self-control to sit down again. "Time presses," he said, "so I'll yield on this one and ask for the answer. Why indeed does a chicken cross the road?"

"Because it's too far to walk around," said Holger.

The giant's curses exploded over him for minutes. He was quite content with that; his whole object was to stall for time, if possible for so long that the first sunrays would fall on his enemy. When the titan finally made a coherent protest, Holger had marshalled enough arguments about the meaning of the terms "question" and "answer" to keep them shouting at each other for half an hour. Bless that college course he'd taken in semantics! He killed ten minutes just reconstructing Bertrand Russell's theory of types.

At last the giant shrugged. "Let it go," he said ominously. "There'll be another night, my friend. Though I think not you will win over me this next time. Go to!"

Holger drew a breath. "What has four legs," he asked, "yellow feathers, lives in a cage, sings and weighs eight hundred pounds?"

The ogre's fist smote the ground so that rocks jumped. "You ask about some unheard-of chimera! That's no riddle, that's a question on natural philosophy."

"If a riddle be a question resolvable by wit, then this is," said Holger. He stole a glance eastward. Was the sky paling, ever so faintly?

The giant cuffed at him, missed, and fell to gnawing his mustache. Obviously the behemoth wasn't very intelligent, Holger decided. Given years in which to mull over a problem, the slowest brain must come up with the answer; but what a human child would have seen in minutes this brute might need hours to solve. He certainly had powers of concentration, though. He sat with eyes squeezed shut, rocking back and forth, mumbling to himself. The fire died low; he became another misshapen shadow.

Hugi tugged at Holger's pants. "Forget not the gold," he whispered avariciously.

"Nor the curse on 't," said Alianora. "For I fear if we win, 'twill no be by wholly honest means."

Holger was too pragmatic to worry about that aspect. Doubtless only a saint could fight evil without being to some extent corrupted by his own deeds. Nevertheless, the giant had come as an unprovoked, cannibalistic aggressor. Hoodwinking him to save Alianora could not be a very heavy sin.

Even so . . . curses were not to be laughed off. Holger felt a chill in his guts. He didn't know why, but an instinct muttered to him that victory over this foe might be as ruinous as defeat.

"Done!" The hideous face opened. "I've found your answer, knight. Two four-hundred-pound canaries!"

Holger sighed. He couldn't expect to win every time. "Okay, Jumbo. Third riddle."

The giant stopped rubbing his hands together. "Don't call me Jumbo!"

"And why not?"

"Because my name is Balamorg. A fearsome name, which many a widow, many an orphan, many a village kicked to flinders, has good cause to know. Call me truly."

"Oh, but you see, where I come from, Jumbo is a term of respect. For hark you——" Holger spun out an improbable story for ten or fifteen minutes. Balamorg interrupted him with a grated command: "The last riddle. Make haste, or I overfall you this instant."

"Heigh-ho. As you wish. Tell me then: what is green, has wheels, and grows around the house?"

"Huh?" The ponderous jaw fell. Holger repeated. "What house?" asked the giant.

"Any house," said Holger.

"Grows, did you say? I told you, questions about some fabulous tree on which wagons cluster like fruit are not true riddles."

Holger sat down and began cleaning his nails with his sword point. It occurred to him that Alfric's magnesium knife might have the same effect as sunlight, when kindled. Or maybe it wouldn't. The total energy output would probably be too small. Still, if he had to fight, he could try the Dagger of Burning. He could now make out his enemy's features, though the fire was burned down to embers.

"The challenges I've given you are common among children in my homeland," he said.

True enough. But Balamorg's wounded ego led to several more

minutes of huffing and puffing. At last, with an angry grunt, he went into his trance of concentration.

Holger sat very still. Alianora and Hugi lay like stones. Even Papillon grew motionless. But their eyes were turned eastward.

And the sky lightened.

After some fraction of eternity, the ogre smote the ground and looked at them. "I give up," he snarled. "The sun pains me already. I must find shelter. What's the answer?"

"Why should I tell you?" Holger rose.

"Because I say so!" The colossus got up too, crouched, lips drawn back from fangs. "Or I'll stamp your wench flat!"

Holger hefted his sword. "Very well," he said. "Grass."

"What?"

"Grass is the answer."

"But grass has no wheels!"

"Oh, I lied about the wheels," said Holger.

Rage ripped from Balamorg in one thunderous bellow. He hurled himself against the knight. Holger skipped back, away from Alianora. Could he keep this monster berserk and witless for another five minutes, and stay alive himself, then— "Nyah, nyah, nyah, can't catch me!" Balamorg's paw snatched at him. He swung his sword with all his force and hewed off a fingertip. Then it was leap and duck, cut and wriggle, taunt to enrage and gasp to breathe.

Until the sun's rim cleared the eastern darkness.

As the first beams touched him, Balamorg screamed. Holger had never heard such agony before. Even while he ran from the toppling mass, he was haunted by the horror of it. The giant hit the ground hard enough to shake boulders loose. He writhed and changed, gruesomely. Then he was silent. The sun fell on a long slab of granite, whose human shape was hardly recognizable but which was still wrapped in skins.

Holger fell to earth also, a roaring in his ears.

He recovered with his head on Alianora's bosom. Her hair and her tears fell on his face like the new sunlight. Hugi capered around the great stone. "Gold, gold, gold!" he cackled. "Ever they giants carry a purseful o' gold. Hurry, man, slit yon sack and make us wealthier nor kings!"

Holger climbed to his feet and approached. "I like this no," said Alianora. "Yet if ye deem it best we take his riches—for sure 'tis we can use some pennies on our faring—then I'll help carry the load, and ask the curse fall on me alone. Oh, my dear!"

Holger waved Hugi aside and stooped by the wallet, a crude draw-string affair. Some coins had already spilled out. They gleamed under his gaze, miniature suns in their own right. Surely, he thought if he put some of this treasure to worthy use, such as building a chapel to good St. George, he could keep the rest unharmed.

What was that smell? Not the stink of the hides, but another, a faint shiff as of rainstorms, under this clear dawn sky. . . . Ozone? Yes. But how come?

"God!" Holger exclaimed. He sprang up, snatched Alianora in his arms and bounded back toward camp. "Hugi! Get away from there! Get away from this whole place! Don't touch a thing if you want to live!"

They were mounted and plunging down the western slope in minutes. Not till they had come miles did Holger feel safe enough to stop. And then he must fob off his companions' demands for an explanation with some weak excuse about the saints vouchsafing him a vision of dire peril. Fortunately his stock stood too high with them for anyone to argue.

But how could he have gotten the truth across? He himself had no real grasp of atomic theory. He'd only learned in college about experiments in transmutation by such men as Rutherford and Lawrence, and about radium burns.

Those tales of a curse on the plunderer of a sun-stricken giant were absolutely correct. When carbon was changed to silicon, you were bound to get a radioactive isotope; and tons of material were involved.

13

AFTERNOON FOUND THEM still descending, but at a gentler pace and in milder air than before lunch. The woodland, oak and beech and scattered firs, revealed signs of man: stumps, second growth, underbrush grazed off, razorback shoats, at last a road of sorts twisting toward the village Alianora expected they could reach today. Exhausted by his encounter with Balamorg, Holger drowsed in the saddle. Birdsong lulled him so that hours went by before he noticed that that was the only noise.

They passed a farmstead. The thatched log house and sheepfolds bespoke a well-to-do owner. But no smoke rose; nothing stirred save a crow that hopped in the empty pens and jeered at them. Hugi pointed to the trail. "As I read the marks, he drave his flocks toonward some days agone," said the dwarf. "Why?"

The sunlight that poured through leafy arches felt less warm to Holger than it had.

At evening they emerged in cleared land. Ripening grainfields stretched ahead, doubtless cultivated by the villagers. The sun had gone down behind the forest, which stood black to the west against a few lingering red gleams. Eastward over the mountains, the first stars blinked forth. There was just enough light for Holger to see a dustcloud a mile or so down the road. He clucked at Papillon and the stallion broke into a weary trot. Alianora, who had amused herself buzzing the bats that emerged with sunset, landed behind the man and resumed her own species. "No sense in alarming yon folk," she said. "Whate'er's their trouble, 'twill ha' made them shy enough."

Hugi's big nose snuffed the air. "They're driving sheep and cattle within the walls," he said. "Eigh, how rank wi' sic smell! And yet's a whiff underneath . . . sweat smells sharper when a man's afeared . . . an' a ghost o' summat else, spooky." He huddled back on the saddlebow, against Holger's mailed breast.

The flocks were considerable. They spilled off the road and across the grain. The boys and dogs who ran about rounding up strays trampled swathes of their own. Some emergency must have forced this, Holger decided. He drew rein as several spearmen challenged him. Squinting through the dusk, he saw the peasants were a sturdy, fair-complexioned folk, bearded and long-haired, clad in rough wadmal coats and cross-gaitered pants. They were too stolid to be made hysterical, but the voices which asked his name were harsh with unease.

"Sir Holger du Danemark and two friends," he said. No use explaining the long-winded truth. "We come in peace, and would like to stay the night."

" 'Olger?" A burly middle-aged man who seemed a leader let his spear down and scratched his head. "Have I not heard that name somewhere before, or its like?"

A murmur went among the men, but no one had an immediate answer and the livestock gave no time for reflection. Holger said quickly, "Whoever bears any such name is not me. I'm a stranger from afar, only passing through."

"Well, sir, welcome to Lourville," said the chief peasant. "I fear you come at an ill time, but Sir Yve will be glad to see you. . . . You, there, head off that bloody-be-damned-to-hell heifer before she ends up in the next duchy! . . . My name's Raoul, Sir 'Olger. Begging your pardon for this hurly-burly."

"What's the trouble?" asked Alianora. "I see ye're housing your beasts within the toon this nicht, which 'twas scarce meant for."

Holger overheard an older man mumble something about these foreign tourists and their scandalously unclad doxies. Someone else hushed him up: "I've heard of her, granther, a swan-may living a bit north and west of Lourville territory. They say she's a kindly one." Holger paid more attention to Raoul:

"Yes, m'lady, we've been grazing everybody's stock in one herd, these last several days, and shutting them in the town after dark. This night, even the people must crowd within the walls; none dare be alone any more, on the outlying garths, when night's fallen. A werewolf goes abroad."

"Hoy, say ye so?" barked Hugi. "A skin-turner?"

"Aye. Much has gone wrong these past years, misfortune after misfortune in every household. My own ax slipped and laid my leg open this spring, and then did the same to my oldest son. We were three weeks abed, right in sowing time. Not a family but has some such tale.

They do say 'tis because of the marshalling in the Middle World beyond the mountains, sorcery grown so strong that its power reaches this far and turns everything awry. So they say." Raoul crossed himself. "I don't know, me. The *loup-garou* is the worst thing thus far. Christ guard us."

"Could it not be a natural wolf that raided your folds?" Alianora asked. "Full oft I've heard folk say someone must be shape-strong, when in fact 'twas but a beast larger and more cunning than most."

"That might have been," said Raoul dourly, "though 'twas hard to see how a natural animal could have broken so many gates or lifted so many latches. Nor do true wolves slay a dozen sheep at a time, for mere sport, like a weasel. But last night the matter was settled. Pier Bigfoot and Berte his wife were in their cottage, three miles within the forest, when the gray one burst through the window and snatched their baby from the cradle. Pier struck with his billhook, and swears the iron passed through the wolf's ribs without doing harm. Then Berte got wild and foolish, and hit the beast with an old silver spoon she had from her grandmother. He dropped the baby—not too badly hurt, by God's grace—and fled out the window. I ask you, is that a natural animal?"

"No," said Alianora, low and frightened.

Raoul spat. "So we'll sleep within the town walls while this danger lasts, and let the wolf prowl untenanted woods. Mayhap we can discover who's turning shape, and burn him." In a gentler tone: "A great pity for Sir Yve, this, just when his daughter Raimberge was readying to travel west and wed the Marchgrave's third son in Vienne. Pray God for a speedy end of our grief."

"Our lord will not be able to entertain you as well as you deserve, Sir 'Olger," added a boy. "He means to walk on the walls this whole night, lest the wolf overleap them. And his lady Blancheflor lies sick abed. But his son and daughter will do what they can."

Holger supposed he should volunteer to help on sentry-go, but he didn't think that after today he could stay awake. As she rode slowly on ahead of the flock, he asked Alianora to explain the menace.

"There be two ways that men take animal shape," she answered. "One is by magic on a common human, as my own feather garb does for me whene'er I make the wish. The other is more darksome. Certain folk be born with twin natures. They need no spell to change form, and each nicht the desire to turn bear, or wild boar, or wolf, or whate'er the animal may be for the person . . . each nicht that desire overwhelms them. And then they run mad. Kind and sensible folk they may be when walking as humans, but as animals they canna cease wreaking harm till the blood thirst is slaked, or till fear o' discovery makes them go back into our form. Whilst beasts, they're nigh impossible to kill, sith wounds knit upon the instant. Only silver pains them, and a silver weapon would slay. But from such they can run swifter nor any true flesh and blood."

"If the, uh, werewolf can't help it, then this local one must be a stranger, not so? A native would have been plaguing the district for years."

"Nay. Methinks as yon crofter said, belike the creature is one o' theirs. For a thin taint o' warg blood micht go unnoticed, unknown, through a lifetime, not being strong enough to reveal itself. 'Tis only o' late, when the witchcraft forces ha' grown so, that the sleeping demon was wakened. I make no doubt the werewolf himself is horror-struck. God help him if e'er the folk learn who he be."

"God help any un yon fear-haggard yokels may decide on for the warg," grunted Hugi.

Holger scowled as he rode on to the gate. It made sense, of the weird sort that prevailed in this universe. Werewolfery . . . what was the word? . . . oh, yes, lycanthropy was probably inherited as a set of recessive genes. If you had the entire set, you were a lycanthrope always and everywhere—and would most likely be killed the first time your father found a wolf cub in his baby's cradle. With an incomplete inheritance, the tendency to change was weaker. It must have been entirely latent and unsuspected in the poor devil of a peasant who bore the curse hereabouts: until the redoubled sorcery in the Middle World blew over the mountains and reinforced whatever body chemistry was involved.

He peered through the gloaming. The village was surrounded by a heavy stockade, with a walkway on which Sir Yve would make his rounds tonight. Inside were jammed narrow wooden houses of two or three stories. The streets that wound among them were mere lanes, stinking from the muck of animals packed in each night. The one on which he entered was a little broader and straighter, but not much. A number of women in long dresses and wimples, shock-haired children, and aproned artisans gaped at him as he passed the gate. Most carried torches that flared and sputtered under the deep-purple sky. Their voices chattered respectfully low as they trailed him.

He stopped near a street leading to one side, a tunnel of blackness walled by the surrounding houses and roofed by their overhanging galleries. Silhouetted above the ridge poles, he could just see the top of a square tower which doubtless belonged to Sir Yve's hall. He leaned toward a husky man, who tugged his forelock and said, "Odo the blacksmith, sir, at your service."

Holger pointed down the alley. "Is this the way to your lord's house?"

"Aye, sir. You, Frodoart, is master at home yet?"

A young man in faded scarlet hose, wearing a sword, nodded. "I did but now leave him, armed cap-a-pie, having a stoup of ale ere he mounts the walls. I am his esquire, Sir Knight. I'll guide you thither. This place is indeed a maze."

Holger removed his helmet, for his hair was dank with sweat after being iron-clad the whole day and the dusk breeze was cool if smelly. He couldn't expect anything lavish at the hall, he realized. Sir Yve de Lourville was obviously not rich—a boondocks knight with a handful of retainers, guarding these environs against bandits and administering a rough justice. Raoul had been filled with civic pride at the daughter's betrothal to a younger son of a minor noble, west in the Empire.

Oh, well, he thought, *something to eat and a place to sleep is all I could make use of anyhow.*

The esquire lifted a torch ahead of him. He patted Papillon for encouragment and started down the lane.

A woman shrieked.

Holger had slapped his helmet back on and drawn his sword before her cry ended. Papillon whirled about. The people drew close to each other; voices rose. The guttering torchlight threw unrestful shadows on the houses across the main street; their upper stories were lost in blackness. Every window was shuttered and door closed, Holger saw. The woman screamed again, behind one of those walls.

A shutter, fastened with an iron bolt, splintered. The shape that sprang forth was long and shaggy, gray as steel in the thick red-shot gloom. It had butted its way out. As it dropped to the street, the muzzle lifted off the chest. Gripped between the jaws there squirmed a naked infant.

"The wolf!" choked the blacksmith. "Holy Mary, we've locked the wolf in with us!"

The child's mother appeared at the window. "It burst in from the rear," she howled witlessly. She stretched her arms toward the beast and them all. "It burst in and snatched Lusiane! There she is, there she is, God strike you down, you men, get my Lusiane back!"

Papillon sped forward. The wolf grinned around the baby. Blood was smeared on her pink skin, but she still cried thinly and struggled. Holger hewed. The wolf wasn't there. Uncannily swift, it had darted between Papillon's legs and was off along the street.

Frodoart the esquire plunged to intercept it. The wolf didn't even break stride as it sprang over him. Ahead was another alley mouth. Holger whirled Papillon around and galloped in pursuit. Too late, though, he thought, too late. Once into that warren of lightless byways, the wolf could devour its prey and turn human again long before any search could—

White wings whirred. Alianora the swan struck with her beak at the warg's eyes. It laid its ears back, twisted aside, and streaked toward the next exit. She swooped in front of it. Like a snowstorm full of buffetings, she halted the runner.

Then Holger had arrived. This far from the torches he was nearly blind, but he could see the great shadowy shape. His sword whistled. He felt the edge cleave meat. Lupine eyes flared at him, cold green and hating. He raised his sword, the blade caught what light there was and he saw it unbloodied. Iron had no power to wound.

Papillon struck with his hoofs, knocked the *loup-garou* to earth and hammered it. The hairy form rolled free, still unhurt. It vanished down the alley. But the child it had dropped lay screaming.

By the time the villagers pounded up, Alianora was human again. She held the girl-baby, smeared with blood and muck, against her. "Och, poor darling, poor lassie, there, there, there. 'Tis over wi' this now. Ye're no too mickle hurt, nobbut a wee bit slashed. Och, 'tis scared ye be. Think how ye can tell your ain children, the best knicht in the world saved ye. There, my love, croodle-doo——" A black-bearded man who must be the father snatched the infant from her, stared a moment, and fell to his knees, shaken with unpracticed weeping.

Holger applied the bulk of Papillon and the flat of his sword to drive the crowd back. "Take it easy," he shouted. "Let's have some order. The kid's all right. You, you, you, come here. I want some torchbearers. Don't stand jabbering. We've got to catch that wolf."

Several men turned green, crossed themselves, and edged away. Odo the blacksmith shook a fist at the alley mouth and said, "How? This mud holds no tracks, nor the paving elsewhere. The fiend will reach his own house unfollowed, and turn back into one of us."

Frodoart regarded the faces which bobbed in and out of moving shadows. "We know he's none of us here," said the esquire above the babble, "nor any of the herders at the gate. That's some help. Let each man remember who stands nigh him."

Hugi tugged Holger's sleeve. "We can track him if ye wish," he said. "Ma nase hairs be atwitch wi' his stink."

Holger wrinkled his own nose. "All I smell is dung and garbage."

"Ah, but ye're no a woods dwarf. Quick, lad, set me doon and let me follow the spoor. But mind ye stay close!"

Holger lifted Alianora back onto his saddle—the child's father kissed her mired feet—and followed Hugi's brown form. Frodoart and Odo walked on either side, torches aloft. Some score of men pressed behind the boldest villagers, armed with knives and staves and spears. If they caught the lycanthrope, Holger thought, it should be possible to hold him by main strength till ropes could be tied on. Then . . . but he didn't like to think of what would follow.

Hugi wound down the lanes for several minutes. He emerged in the marketplace, which was cobbled and showed a little lighter under the stars. "Aye, clear as mustard, the scent," he called. "Naught i' the world has a stench like a werebeast in his animal shape." Holger wondered if glandular secretions were responsible. The stones rang hollow under Papillon's shoes.

The street they took off the market square was also more or less paved, and comparatively wide. Here and there were lighted houses, but Hugi ignored the people inside. Straight he ran, until a cry went up at Holger's back.

"No!" groaned Frodoart. "Not my master's hall!"

14

THE KNIGHT'S DWELLING stood on a plaza of its own, opposite the church and otherwise hemmed in with houses. Kitchen and stables were separate buildings. The hall was unimpressive, a thatched wooden affair not much larger than the average bungalow in Holger's world. It was T-shaped, with the left branch of the cross-arm rising in the tower he had noticed before. The front was at the end of the T's upright, and closed. Light gleamed from shuttered windows; dogs clamored in the stables.

Hugi approached the iron-studded door. "Straight in here the warg fled," he declared.

"With my master's family alone!" Frodoart tried the latch. "Barred. Sir Yve! Can you hear me? Are you well?"

"Odo, cover the rear," snapped Holger. "Alianora, get aloft and report anything unusual." He rode up to the door and knocked with the pommel of his sword. The blacksmith gathered several men and ran around in back. Hugi followed. More people streamed into the square. By fugitive yellow torch gleams, Holger recognized some of the herders among them. Raoul the peasant pushed through the crowd to join him, spear in hand.

The knocking boomed hollow. "Are they dead in there?" sobbed Frodoart. "Burst this down! Are you men or dogs, standing idle when your lord needs you?"

"Are there any back doors?" Holger asked. The blood thudded in his temples. He had no fear of the werewolf, nor even any sense of strangeness. This was *right:* the work for which he had been born.

Hugi threaded a way among legs and rattled his stirrup for attention. "No other door, but windows eneugh, each locked tighter nor the last," the dwarf reported. "Yet the warg ha' no left this bigging. I snuffed everywhere aboot. E'en had he jumped from yon tower, I'd ha' covered the ground where he maun land. Noo all ways oot are blockaded. We ha' him trapped."

Holger glanced around. The villagers had stopped milling; they surrounded the hall, packed and very still. Torchlight fluttered across a woman's frightened pale face, a man's sweating hairiness, a startling gleam of eyeballs in shadow. Weapons bristled above, spears, axes, bills, scythes, flails. "What about servants?" he asked Frodoart.

"None in there, sir," said the esquire. "The house servants are townsfolk, who go home after dark, leaving only old Nicholas to do for the family. I see him yonder, as well as the stablehands. . . . Get us inside!"

"I'm about to, if you'll give me some room."

Frodoart and Raoul cleared a space with well-meant if brutal efficiency. Holger stroked Papillon's mane and murmured, "Okay, boy, let's see what we're good for." He reared the horse. The forefeet smashed against the panels. Once, twice, thrice, then the bolt tore loose and the door sprang open.

Holger rode into a single room. The dirt floor was strewn with rushes. Above the built-in benches along the walls hung weapons and hunting trophies. Dusty battle banners stirred among the rafters. Sconced candles lit the place fairly well, showing it empty down to a doorway at the end. Beyond must lie the crossbar of the T, private apartments of Sir Yve and his family. A yell rose from the men who crowded behind Holger. For that doorway was blocked by a form shining steely in the candleglow.

"Who are you?" The man waved a sword above his shield. "What is this outrage?"

"Sir Yve!" exclaimed Frodoart. "The wolf has not harmed you?"

"What wolf? What the devil are you up to? You, sirrah, what excuse have you for forcing your way in? Are you a blood-enemy of mine? If not, by God's death, I can soon make you one!"

Holger dismounted and walked close. Sir Yve de Lourville was a tall, rather thin man with a melancholy horse face and drooping gray mustaches. He wore more elaborate armor than the Dane, a visored casque, corselet, brassards, elbow-pieces, cuisses, greaves, plus chain-mail. His shield bore a wolf's head erased, sable on barry of six, gules and argent, which Holger found eerily suggestive. If some distant ancestor had been a full-fledged *loup-garou*, the fact might be hushed up by later generations, but could linger as a traditional coat of arms. . . .

"I'm called Holger du Danemark. The werewolf appeared before

me as well as many other people. Only by God's mercy did we rescue
the baby it had stolen. Now we've tracked it here."

"Aye," said Hugi. "The trail runs clear to yersel'."

A gasp went among the commoners, like the first sigh of wind
before a storm.

"You lie, dwarf! I've sat here this eventide. No beast entered." Sir
Yve jabbed his sword toward Holger. "None are present but my lady,
who's ill, and my two children. If you claim aught else, you must prove
it on my body."

His voice wobbled. He wasn't a very good blusterer. Raoul was the
first to snarl, "If matters be as you say, Sir Yve, then one of your own
must be the fiend."

"I forgive you this time," said Sir Yve frantically. "I know you're
overwrought. But the next man who speaks such words will dangle from
the gallows."

Frodoart stood with the tears whipping down his cheeks. "Dwarf,
dwarf, how can you be sure?" he groaned.

Sir Yve seized upon the question. "Aye, who would you trust—this
misshapen mannikin and this hedge-knight, or your lord who has warded
you all these years?"

A boy of fourteen or so appeared behind him, slender and blond.
He had put on a helmet, snatched sword and shield, in obvious haste,
for otherwise he wore the colorful tunic and hose which was the local
equivalent of a white tie. Of course, thought Holger faintly, in an outpost
of civilization every aristocrat dressed for dinner.

"Here I am, father," panted the youth. His green eyes narrowed at
Holger. "I am Gui, son of Yve de Lourville, and though not yet knighted
I call you false and defy you to battle." It would have been more im-
pressive if his voice hadn't developed an adolescent crack, but was
nonetheless touching.

*Sure, why not? The lycanthrope is a perfectly decent person, except
when the skin-turning rage is upon him.*

Holger sighed and put away his blade. "I don't want to fight," he
said. "If your people don't believe me, I'll go away."

The commoners shifted about, stared at the floor, back at Holger
and Yve. Frodoart aimed a furtive kick at Hugi, who dodged. Then Odo
the smith came in the door and forced a path for Alianora. "The swan-
may would speak," he trumpeted. "The swan-may who saved Lusiane.
Be quiet, there, you muttonheads, ere I clobber you."

A hush fell until they could hear the dogs howl outside. Holger saw
Raoul's knuckles whiten about his spear. A little man in priestly robe
went to his knees, crucifix in hand. Gui's beardless jaw dropped. Sir

Yve crouched as if wounded. No eye left Alianora. She stood slender and straight, the candleglow shimmering in the coppery-brown hair, and said:

"Some o' ye must ken my name, I who dwell by Lake Arroy. I mislike brags, but they'll tell ye in places closer to my home, like Tarn-berg and Cromdhu, how many strayed children I've fetched back from the woods and how I got Mab hersel' to take off the curse she laid on Philip the miller. I ha' kenned Hugi my whole life, and vouch for him. We've none o' us aught to gain by slander. 'Tis your fortune that the finest knicht who ever lived has come by in time to free ye from the warg ere it takes a human life. Hearken to him, I say!"

An old man tottered forth. He blinked half-blind and said into the stillness, "Mean you this is the Defender?"

"What are you talking about?" asked Holger with some dismay.

"The Defender . . . he that shall return in our greatest need . . . the legend my grandsire told me gives not his name, but are you him, Lord Knight, are you him?"

"No——" Holger's protest was drowned in a rumble like the in-coming tide. Raoul sprang forward with spear poised.

"By heaven, he's no master of mine who snatches children!" the peasant yelled. Frodoart swung at him with his sword, but weakly. The blow was turned by the spearshaft. A moment later four men had pinned the esquire down.

Sir Yve leaped at Holger. The Dane got his weapon out barely in time to parry the blow. He struck back so hard he cracked the other's shield-rim. Yve staggered. Holger knocked the sword from his grasp. Two peasants caught their overlord's arms. Gui tried to attack, but a pitchfork pricked his breast and drove him back against the wall.

"Get these people under control, Odo, Raoul!" Holger gasped. "Don't let them hurt anyone. You, you, you." He pointed out several big eager-looking youths. "Guard this doorway. Don't let anybody past. Alianora, Hugi, come with me."

He sheathed his sword again and hurried through. A corridor pan-eled in carven wood ran transversely to the main room, a door at either end and one in the middle. Holger tried that one. It swung open on a chamber hung with skins and a moth-eaten tapestry. The light of tapers fell on a woman who lay in the canopied bed. Her graying hair was lank around a handsome flushed face; she snuffled and sneezed into a handkerchief. A bad case of influenza, Holger decided. The girl who had sat next to the bed and now rose was more interesting—only about sixteen, but with a pleasant figure, long yellow tresses, blue eyes, tip-tilted nose and attractive mouth. She wore a simple pullover dress, gathered with a golden-buckled belt.

Holger bowed. "Forgive the intrusion, madame, mademoiselle. Necessity compels."

"I know," said the girl unsteadily. "I heard."

"The Demoiselle Raimberge, are you not?"

"Yes, daughter to Sir Yve. My mother Blancheflor." The lady in question wiped her nose and looked at Holger with fear blurred by physical misery. Raimberge wrung her small hands. "I cannot believe what you think, sir. That one of us is . . . is that thing——" She bit back tears; she was a knight's daughter.

"The scent gaes hither," said Hugi.

"Could either of you have witnessed the beast's entry?" asked Holger.

Blancheflor shook her head. Raimberge explained: "We were separate in our chambers, Gui in his and I in mine, readying to sup, my lady mother sleeping here. Our doors were closed. My father was in the main hall. When I heard the tumult, I hastened to comfort my mother."

"Then Yve himself must be the warg," Alianora said.

"No, not my father!" Raimberge whispered. Blancheflor covered her face. Holger turned on his heel. "Let's look about," he said.

Gui's room was at the foot of the tower, to whose top a stair led. It was crammed with boyish souvenirs. Raimberge's was at the opposite end of the corridor, with a chestful of trousseau, a spinning wheel, and whatever else pertained to a young girl of shabby-genteel birth. All three rear rooms had windows, and Hugi couldn't follow the scent in detail. He said it was everywhere; the wolf had haunted this part of the house night after night. Not that anyone need see the apparition. It could use a window for exit and re-entrance, when everybody else was asleep.

"One o' three," said Alianora. Her voice was unhappy.

"Three?" Hugi lifted his brows. "Why think ye the lady canna be the beast? Would she no ha' her health as soon's she turned wolf?"

"Would she? I dinna know. The wargs are no so common that I e'er heard talk o' wha' happens when one falls ill. . . . Four, then. One o' four."

Holger returned glum to the feasting chamber. Raoul and Odo had established a sort of order. The men stood around the walls, Papillon by the main door. Yve and Gui sat in the high seat, bound hand and foot. Frodoart huddled beneath, disarmed but otherwise unhurt. The priest told his beads.

"Well!" Raoul turned fiercely on the newcomers. "Who's the cursed one?"

"We dinna know," said Alianora.

Gui spat toward Holger. "When first I saw you helmetless, I didn't imagine you a knight," the boy taunted. "Now when I see you bursting in on helpless women, I know you're not."

Raimberge entered behind Hugi. She went to her father and kissed his cheek. With a glance that swept the hall, she called: "Worse than beasts, you, who turn on your own liege lord!"

Odo shook his head. "No, ma'm'selle," he said. "The lord who fails his people is none. I got little ones of my own. I'll no hazard them being eaten alive."

Raoul struck the wainscot with his spear butt. "Silence, there!" he barked. "The wolf dies this night. Name him, Sir 'Olger. Or her. Name us the wolf."

"I——" Holger felt suddenly ill. He wet his lips.

"We canna tell," said Hugi.

"So." Raoul scowled at the grim rough-clad assembly. "I feared that. Well, will the beast confess himself? I'll slay him mercifully, with a silver knife in the heart."

"Iron will do, while he's human," said Odo. "Come, now. Speak up. I'd not like to put you to torture."

Frodoart stirred. "Before you do that," he said, "you must peel my hands off your throat." They ignored him.

"If none will confess," said Raoul, "then best they all die. We've the priest here to shrive them."

Gui fought back a sob. Raimberge grew death-still. They heard Blancheflor cough at the dark end of the house.

Yve seemed to shrink into himself. "Very well," he said, tonelessly. "I am the wolf."

"No!" Gui shrilled. "I am!"

Raimberge stood for a moment, until a hard smile touched her lips. "They both lie nobly," she said. "The skin-turner is myself, though, good folk. And you need not slay me, only guard me until time that I go to my wedding in Vienne. That far from the lands of Faerie, I'll be beyond range of the powers which forced me to change."

"Believe her not," said Gui. Yve shook his head violently. A hoarse call might have been Blancheflor taking the blame on herself.

"This gets us no further," said Raoul. "We can't risk letting the *loup-garou* go free. Father Valdabrun, will you ready the last rites for this family?"

Holger drew sword and sprang before the high seat. "You'll not kill the innocent while I'm alive," said a voice and a will he recognized with amazement as his own.

The blacksmith Odo clenched his fists. "I'd be loath to overfall you, Sir 'Olger," he said, "but if I must for my children, I must."

"If you are the Defender," said Raoul, "then name us our enemy."

The stiffness fell again, stretched close to breaking. Holger felt the three pairs of eyes burn at his back: careworn Yve, ardent Gui, Raimberge who had been so hopeful. He heard the wheezing of the sick woman. *O Christ who cast out demons, aid me now*. Only afterward did he realize he had said his first conscious prayer since childhood.

What came to the forefront of his mind was something else, the workaday engineer's approach. He was no longer sure of his old belief that all problems in life were practical problems. But this one was. A question of rational analysis. He was no detective, but neither was the warg a professional criminal. There must be——

It blazed in him. "By the Cross, yes!" he shouted.

"What? What? What?" Men started to their feet. Holger waved his sword aloft. The words spilled from him. He didn't know himself what he would say next, he was thinking aloud in a roar, but they heard him with wonder:

"Look, the one we're after is shape-strong by birth. He doesn't need any magical skin, like the swan-may here. But then his clothes can't change with him, can they? So he must go forth naked. Frodoart told me, a moment before the wolf showed up, he'd just left his master full-armed in the hall. And alone. Though even with help Sir Yve couldn't have gotten out of that armor, and back into it afterward, in the few minutes he had. So he's not the warg.

"Gui tried to plead guilty too, to save whoever else was. But he'd already scuttled himself. He mentioned having seen me helmetless. I was for one minute, when I stopped to inquire my way here. I put the helmet back on when the racket started. The wolf couldn't have seen that. He—no, she—she was inside a house. She broke in through the rear door and escaped out a front window, which had been shuttered. The only way Gui could have seen me bareheaded in the torchlight was from the top of the tower above his room. I noticed it sticking over the roofs. He must have gone up to watch the flocks being driven in. So he was not anywhere near the place we saw the warg.

"Lady Blancheflor——" He stopped. How on earth, on all the Earths, could he explain the germ theory of disease? "Lady Blancheflor has been sick, with an illness that the dog tribe doesn't get. If changing into a wolf did not make her well, then she'd be too weak to dash around as I saw the animal do. If the change did make her well, the, uh, the agent causing the disease couldn't live in her animal body. She wouldn't have a fever and a runny nose at this moment, would she? In either case, she's eliminated."

Raimberge cowered back against the wall. Her father made a broken noise and twisted about, trying to reach her with his bound hands. "No, no, no," he keened. A noise like the wolf itself lifted from the commons. They began to edge close, one mass of hands and weapons.

The girl dropped on all fours. Her face writhed and altered, horrible to watch. "Raimberge!" Holger bawled. "Don't! I won't let them——" Raoul's spear stabbed for her. Holger knocked it aside and cut the shaft across with his sword.

Raimberge howled. Alianora dropped to her knees and caught the half-altered body in her arms. "Nay," she pleaded. "Nay, my sister, come back. He swears he'll save ye." The jaws snapped at her. She got her forearm crosswise into the mouth, forcing lips over fangs so the wolf couldn't bite. She wrestled the creature to a standstill. "Lassie, lassie, we mean ye well."

Holger waded into the mob. Turmoil broke loose. But after he had knocked several down, with a fist or the flat of his blade, they quieted. They snarled and grumbled, but the man in the hauberk overawed them.

He turned to Raimberge. She had resumed her human form and lay weeping in Alianora's embrace. "I didn't want to be. I didn't want to. It came on me. And, and, and I was so afraid they'd burn me— Is my soul lost, Father Valdabrun? I th-think I must be in hell already. The way those babies screamed——"

Holger exchanged a look with the priest. "Sick," said the Dane. "She's not evil of her own will. She can't help it."

Yve stared like a blind man. "I had thought it might be her," he mumbled. "When the wolf ran in, past me, and I knew where Blanche-flor and Gui were—I barred the door. I hoped, if this could only pass over until she departed——"

Holger squared his shoulders. "I don't see why not," he answered. "The idea is perfectly sound, as I understand the matter. Let her get far enough away, and the Middle World influence will be too weak to affect her. Till then, of course, you'll have to keep her under restraint. She's sorry now, but I don't think that'll last."

"At dawn it will, when her human soul awakens," said the priest. "Then she will indeed need comforting."

"Well," said Holger, "nothing too serious ever happened. Her father can pay compensation to the people who suffered loss and the parents whose kids were injured. Start her off for Vienne as soon as possible. I daresay a hundred miles would be quite far enough for safety. No one in the Empire has to know."

Raoul, with a black eye, threw himself at Sir Yve's feet while Odo, with a bloody nose, fumbled to release the knight and his son. "Master, forgive us," the peasant begged.

Yve made a weary smile. "I fear 'tis I must ask your forgiveness. And yours above all, Sir 'Olger."

Raimberge lifted her wet face. "Take me off," she stammered. "I, I, I feel the darkness returning. Lock me away till dawn." She held out her arms for the ropes taken off her father. "Tomorrow, Sir Knight, I can truly thank you . . . who saved my soul from hell."

Frodoart embraced Holger's knees. "The Defender is come," he said.

"Oh, Lord!" protested the Dane. "Please, lay off that nonsense. I mean, I hate emotional scenes and I only came here to bum a meal. But could I have some wine first?"

15

BESIDES THE NEED for haste, to get expert advice before Morgan le Fay thought up a new devilment, Holger felt embarrassed in Lourville. Yve's family were grateful and so forth, but they didn't need further intrusions on their privacy at such a difficult time. The commoners were rather overwhelming; he couldn't venture out of the house without being mobbed by his admirers. Lady Blancheflor asked that he lay hands on her, and within hours she was on her feet. She'd been due to recover anyway, her influenza past the crisis, but Holger could foresee every case of measles and rheumatism for ten miles around being brought to him.

So, what with one thing and another, he only stayed one day, and made an early start on the next. Sir Yve insisted on presenting Alianora with a horse, and this was welcome. Some money would have been even more welcome, but of course no belted knight could bring up so crass a subject.

The next several days were pleasant. They drifted through hills and valleys and forests, sheltering when it rained, pausing at lakes to fish and swim. Now and then they glimpsed the white shape of a woods-fay, or a griffin hot and golden against the sun; but the Middle Worlders let them alone.

To be sure, Alianora, though a fine and lovely girl, had some draw-backs as a traveling companion. The self-cleaning, self-renewing prop-erties of her swan tunic disconcerted Holger: too much like an actual skin growing on her. Then she peeled it innocently off at the first swim-ming hole and disconcerted him a good deal more. Her forest friends showed up from time to time, and a squirrel with an offering of fruits was okay; but when a lion stalked into camp and laid a fresh-killed deer at her feet, Holger's nerves didn't untwist for half an hour afterward. Worse was the moral necessity of giving her a full and fair account of himself, his origin and intentions. Not that she wasn't quick to understand—but——

The real trouble was her own attitude toward him. Damn it, he did not want to compromise himself with her. A romp in the hay with someone like Meriven or Morgan was one thing. Alianora was something else. An affair with her wouldn't be good for either party, when he meant to leave this world the first chance he got. But she made it hard for him to remain a gentleman. She was so shyly and pathetically hoping for an affair.

One evening he drew Hugi aside. He'd just spent an hour kissing Alianora goodnight, and had needed all his willpower—or won't power—to stop at that and pack her off to sleep. "Look," he said, "you know what's going on with me and her."

"Aye, so I do," grinned the dwarf. "And a guid thing 'tis. She's dwelt too long wi' no near friends save beasties and the wee folk."

"But . . . but you warned me to behave myself with her."

"That were afore I kenned ye well. Noo methinks ye're a richt guid man for her; and the lassie needs a man. She and ye could reign o'er us in the woods. We'd be glad o' ye."

"Good grief! You're no help whatsoever."

"I been as helpfu' as could be," said Hugi in an injured tone. "Ye dinna know hoo oft I turned ma face, or wandered into the woods, to leave ye twa alane."

"That's not what—— Oh, never mind."

Holger lit his pipe and stared gloomily into the fire. He wasn't any Don Juan. He couldn't understand why one woman after another, in this world, should throw herself at him. Meriven and Morgan had had good practical reasons, but he wasn't too dense to realize they had enjoyed their work more than usual. Alianora had quite simply fallen in love with him. Why? He had no illusions about his own irresistibility.

But of course that alter ego of his could be another story. He imagined that his slow return to forgotten habits showed in numberless subtle ways which transformed the total impression he made. What had he been like, this knight of the hearts and lions?

Well, let's see. Figure it out on the basis of what had happened hitherto. Obviously a mighty warrior, which was what counted most in this world. A gusty, good-natured bruiser, not especially nimble-witted, but likeable. Something of an idealist, presumably: Morgan had spoken of his defending Law even if he stood to gain more from Chaos. He must have had a way with the ladies, or so wise a jade as she would hardly have taken him off to Avalon. And . . . and . . . that seemed to be all he could deduce. Or remember?

No, wait, Avalon. Holger looked at his right hand. That same hand had rested on a balustrade of green malachite, whose top was set with silver figures that had jewels in their centers. He remembered how the sun had fallen on the back of his hand, turning the hair to gold wires against the brown skin, and how the silver under his palm was warmer than the stone, and how the rubies glowed crimson. Straight down below the balustrade tumbled a cliff, which was of glass. From above he could see how the grottos broke light into a million rainbow shards, spraying the light outward again, hot sparks of red and gold and violet. The sea beneath had been so dark it was almost purple, with foam of amazing snowy whiteness where the cliff plowed the water . . . for Avalon stayed never in one place, the island floated over the western ocean in a haze of its own magic. . . .

No more would come to mind. Holger sighed and composed himself for sleep.

After a week or so—he lost count of days—they left the wilderness and entered lands where the forest was thinned to copses. Grainfields billowed yellow across the hills. Shaggy little horses and cows pastured behind rail fences. The peasant homes grew numerous, mostly of rammed earth in this district, clustered in hamlets amid the cultivated acres. Here and there could be seen a stockaded wooden castle. The up-to-date ones of stone lay westward, where the Holy Empire held full sway. The mountains Holger had crossed, and the Faerie wall of dusk, were quite lost to sight. Northward, however, he saw the dim blue line of a much higher range, three of whose snowpeaks seemed to float pale and disembodied in the sky. Hugi said the Middle World lay beyond those too. No wonder the men hereabouts always went armed, even when working in the fields; no wonder the elaborate hierarchical civilization of the Empire was discarded for a frontier informality. The knights who put the travelers up two evenings in succession were unlettered, rough-fisted Western marshal types, though friendly enough and avid for news.

Toward sunset of their third day in the farmlands they entered Tarnberg, which Alianora said was the nearest thing to a city in the whole eastern half of the duchy. But its castle stood vacant. The baron had fallen with his sons in battle against heathen raiders from the north, his lady had gone west to her Imperial kinfolk, and no successor had yet arrived. It was a part of the general bad luck in the last few years, the radiation of Chaos as the Middle Worlders readied their powers. Now the Tarnberg men posted their own guard on the wooden walls, and governed themselves by an improvised council of estates.

As he rode in Holger saw a cobbled street where children, dogs, and pigs played, winding between half-timbered houses toward a market square where stood a wooden church rather like a Norwegian stave kirk. Papillon stepped through a noisy clutter of workmen and housewives, who gaped, made clumsy bows, but didn't venture to address him. There was no sense in advertising himself, so he had covered his shield. Alianora, who rode ahead with Hugi, was well known, and Holger heard how they called to her.

"Hoy, there, swan-may, what brings you hither?"

"Who's the knight?"

"What's new in the woods, swan-may?"

"What news from Charlemont? Saw you my cousin Hersent?"

"Know you aught of the hosting in Faerie?" An anxious voice, that; folk who heard crossed themselves.

"Is't a lord you bring to ward us?"

The girl smiled and waved, though not quite happily. She didn't like so many walls or people around.

She guided Holger to a house even narrower and more irregularly cornered than average. A signboard hung from the gallery, above the door. Holger read the florid script.

MARTINUS TRISMEGISTUS
Magister Magici
Spells, Charms, Prophecies, Healing, Love Potions
Blessings, Curses, Ever-Filled Purses
Special rates for parties

"Hm," he said. "Looks like an enterprising chap."

"Och, indeed," said Alianora. "He's also Tarnberg's apothecary, dentist, scribe, dowser, and horse doctor."

She swung lithely down with a flash of long bare legs. Holger followed, looping the reins to a post. A few rough-looking men lounged across the way, their gaze intent on the animals and gear. "Keep an eye on things, Hugi," he said.

"Why, if any tried to steal Papillon, I'd bewail 'em," answered the dwarf.

"*Ja*, that's what I'm afraid of," said Holger.

He was doubtful about entrusting his secret, such as it was, to this horse-and-buggy wizard. But Alianora had recommended the fellow highly, and he didn't know where else to turn.

A bell jangled as they entered the shop. The place was dark and dusty. Shelves and tables were heaped with a jackdaw's nest of bottles, flasks, mortars, alembics, retorts, huge leather-bound books, skulls, stuffed animals, and Lord knew what else. An owl on a perch hooted, a cat leaped from underfoot.

"Coming, coming, good sir, one moment, please," called a high thin voice. Master Martinus trotted from the back rooms and rubbed his hands together. He was a small man in a shabby black robe on which the zodiacal symbols had faded from much laundering. His round bald head showed a wispy beard and weak blinking eyes; his smile was timid. "Ah, how do you do, sir, how do you do? What can I do for you?" Peering closer: "Why, it's the little swan maiden. Come in, my dear, do come in. But of course, you're already in, are you not? Yes, yes, so you are."

"We've a task for ye, Martinus," said Alianora. "It may task ye in truth, but we've none other wha' micht help."

"Well, well, well, I shall do what I can, my dear, and you too, good sir. I shall do what I can. Excuse me." Martinus wiped the dust off a parchment hung on the wall, which was one way of drawing Holger's attention to it. The writing thereon declared that whereas Martinus filius Holofii had met the standards set by the examining board, etc., etc., now therefore by virtue of the powers vested in me by the Regents of the University of Rhiannon, I do hereby confer upon him the degree of Magister in the field of Magic, with all privileges and obligations thereunto pertaining, etc., etc.

"I'm afraid I can't——" Holger was about to explain he had no money, but Alianora dug an elbow in his ribs.

"There be frichtful secrets in this yarn," she said quickly. " 'Tis no for any common hill-wizard to scorch his soul wi'." She gave the magician such a smile that even Holger, who stood on its fringes, felt sandbagged. "So I brocht the knicht hither to ye."

"And very wisely, my girl, very wisely, if I do say so myself. Come in, please, come into my office and we will discuss your problem." Martinus puttered ahead of them to a cubicle as grimy and cluttered as the shop. He dumped books from chairs, muttering something apologetic about his housekeeper, and piped aloud, "Wine! Bring wine for three." After a short silence: "Hi, there! I say, do wake up! Wine for three."

Holger lowered himself into one of the chairs, which creaked alarmingly under his weight. Alianora poised on the edge of another, flickering her eyes about like a snared bird. Martinus found a third seat, crossed his legs, made a bridge of his fingers, and said, "Now, sir, what seems to be your difficulty?"

"Well, uh," said Holger, "well, it all began back when—oh, hell, I hardly know where to begin."

"Would you like a couch to lie on?" asked Martinus solicitously.

A bottle and three dirty goblets floated in and landed on the table. "About time," grumbled the sorcerer. After a moment, when the invisible servant had presumably left, he went on, "I declare, there is no decent help to be had these days. None. That sprite, now, he is quite impossible. Improbable, at least," he qualified. "Not like when I was a boy. Such classes knew their place then. And as for herbs, and mummy, and powdered toad, why, they just don't put the sort of stuff into them they used to. And the prices! My dear sir, you'll scarcely believe it, but only last Michaelmas——"

Alianora coughed. "Oh, pardon me," said Martinus. "I rambled. Bad habit, rambling. Must make a note not to ramble." He poured the wine and offered it around. It was drinkable. "Proceed, good sir, I pray you. Say what you will."

Holger sighed and launched into his story. Martinus surprised him with questions and comments as shrewd as Duke Alfric's had been. When Holger recounted his stay with Mother Gerd, the wizard shook his head. "I know of her," he said. "Not a good sort. Not surprising you got into trouble. She traffics with black magic. It's these unlicensed practitioners who give the whole profession a bad name. But do go on, sir."

At the end Martinus pursed his lips. "A strange tale," he said. "Yes, I think your supposition is right. You are the crux of a very large matter indeed."

Holger trembled as he leaned forward. "Who am I?" he asked. "Who bears three hearts and three lions?"

"I'm afraid I don't know, Sir Holger. I suspect you are, or were, some great man in the western lands, France for example." Martinus looked pedantic. "Are you familiar with the mystical geography? Well, you see, the world of Law—of man—is hemmed in with strangeness, like an island in the sea of the Middle World. Northward live the giants, southward the dragons. Here in Tarnberg we are close to the eastern edge of human settlement and know a trifle about such kingdoms as Faerie and Trollheim. But news travels slowly and gets dissipated in the process. So we have only vague, distorted rumors of the western realms—not merely the Middle World domains out in the western ocean, like Avalon, Lyonesse, and Huy Braseal, but even the human countries such as France and Spain. Thus, although this knight of hearts and lions, who seems in some manner to be yourself, may be a household name in that part of the world, I cannot identify him. Nor do I think the information is in my books, though I really must catalogue my library one of these days.

"However"—he grew earnest and lost some of his fussiness—"in a general way, I think I can see what has happened. This western knight would have been too great a foe for Chaos to meet. Quite likely he was one of the Chosen, like Carl or Arthur or their greatest paladins. I do not mean a saint, but a warrior whom God gave more than common gifts and then put under a more than common burden. The knights of the Round Table and of Carl's court are long dead, but another champion may have taken their place. So before Chaos could hope to advance, this man had to be gotten out of the way.

"Morgan may well have done that herself, by burying his past life in him beyond the aid of any ordinary spell, turning him into a child, and projecting him into your other world, in hopes that he would not return until Chaos had irretrievably won. Why she did not merely assassinate him, I cannot say. Perhaps she didn't have the heart to. Or perhaps, being one of the Chosen, he was shielded by a greater Power than hers.

"In any event, I believe he was returned here at the crucial moment. Direct divine intervention seems unlikely; with all due respect, sir, I doubt if you are quite in a state of grace as yet, and certainly the spell on your mind remains. No, I think Morgan did not realize that unity of creation which you say you speculated about. At the moment of greatest need, the champion *had* to return. And now the Middle World is using its arts and strength to block him. Or you, as the case may be," Martinus finished anticlimactically. "This is only a theory, my dear sir. Only a theory. But I flatter myself that it does fit the known facts."

Holger hunched his shoulders. It was an eerie situation. He didn't like being a chess piece.

No, he wasn't that. He was free. Too free. He embodied a power he did not know anything about and could not handle. Oh, blast and damn! Why did this have to happen to him, out of every soul alive?

"Can you send me back?" he asked tautly.

Alianora drew a sharp breath, then looked away. She'd known he wanted to return, thought Holger with a tinge of remorse, but she'd ignored the fact, lived in some kind of dream, until this moment.

Martinus shook his head. "No, sir, I fear the task is too great for me. Most likely too great for anyone, mortal or Middle Worlder. If my guess is correct, then you have not only been caught up in the struggle between Law and Chaos, you are an integral part thereof."

He sighed. "Perhaps once," he said, "when I was young and gay and arrogant, I might have tried to oblige you. I'd attempt anything in those days. You have no idea what student pranks can be till you've seen a magicians' college. . . . But I have learned my limitations. I fear I can give you little help, nor even much advice."

"But what should I do?" asked Holger helplessly. "Where should I go?"

"I cannot tell. And yet—yet there is that item of the sword Cortana. Tales come out of the west, but so unwontedly clear and fulsome that I think the events concerned may have happened rather closer to here. The story is of a sword named Cortana, of the same steel as Joyeuse, Durindal, and Excalibur; and the story is also that a holy man, a veritable saint, laid his blessing upon Cortana, that in the hands of its rightful owner it might bulwark Christendie now that those other great weapons are gone with their masters. But later, the tale says, the sword was stolen away and buried in some distant place by the minions of . . . Morgan le Fay? You see, they could not destroy it, but with the help of heathen men who could ignore the sacredness, they hid Cortana away lest it be used against them."

"Should I try to find it, then?"

"A dangerous business, young man. Yet I see nothing else which can long protect you against your foes. Tell you what." Martinus tapped Holger's knee. "Tell you what I'll do. I'll use my powers, and some have been kind enough to call 'em not inconsiderable, to try and find out who you are and where the sword is hidden. Its aura would make it perceptible to such airy sprites as I can summon. Yes, that seems the best course."

"Thank ye more than I can tell," said Alianora. The prospect of danger didn't seem to bother her, in her relief that Holger wasn't going to be whisked away the next minute.

"I fear I've no guest space," said Martinus, "but there's a tavern where you can stay overnight. Tell the landlord I sent you, and—hm, no, I'd forgotten about that bill of his. Well, come back tomorrow. . . . Oh, yes. Would you like a disguise against the Saracen? I have some good disguises, very reasonably priced."

"The Saracen?" Holger exclaimed.

"What? Didn't I tell you? Bless my soul, so I didn't. Clean forgot. Getting absent-minded. Must remember to whip up a memory-strengthening spell. Oh, yes, the Saracen you'd heard was looking for you. He's in town too."

16

A SEARCH OF HIS BOOKS confirmed Martinus' belief that he had no cantrips powerful enough to lift the veil from Holger's mind. But with a few passes and some foul-smelling fumes, he provided the Dane a new face. A mirror showed Holger his own countenance turned dark and rough-looking; his hair and the short yellow beard he had grown were now black, his eyes brown. Alianora sighed. "I like ye better as ye were," she said.

"When you wish to resume your natural appearance, call on Belgor Melanchos and this will whiff away," said Martinus. "But beware of getting too close to any sacred object. The sword Cortana, for instance, will dissolve the spell too. Not that the sin involved in this particular thaumaturgy is more than venial, but it does have pagan elements, and the holy influence— Anyway, keep your distance from blessed things. Inverse square law, you know."

"Better fix up my horse," said Holger. "He's rather distinctive too."

"My dear fellow!" sputtered Martinus.

"Please," purred Alianora. She waved her lashes at him.

"Oh, very well, very well. Bring him in. But mind he behaves himself."

Papillon almost filled the shop. He emerged as a big chestnut destrier. While he was at it, Martinus also transformed Holger's shield. When asked what new device he wanted, the Dane could only think of *Ivanhoe*, so he got an uprooted tree. He himself, because of being involved in the illusion, could only see these changes in a mirror.

"Come back tomorrow and I'll tell you what I've been able to learn," said the magician. "Not before noon, mind you. These backwoodsmen keep ungodly hours."

On the way to the inn they passed the church. Holger stopped his horse. He wanted to go in and pray. But no, he dared not with this disguise. More of the unknown knight? He must have been pious in his fashion. It was hard to fare back to darkness without having received the Host. . . . Holger kicked Papillon into a trot.

By this time night had fallen and they groped through unlighted streets to the tavern. A plump, cheerful-looking man met them in the courtyard. "Lodging for yourselves? Aye, sir, I've a fine room which has even pillowed crowned heads."

Which I hope didn't lie uneasy because of bedbugs, Holger thought. "Two rooms," he said.

"Oh, I'll snark in the stable wi' the horses," leered Hugi.

"We still want two rooms," said Holger.

As they dismounted, Alianora leaned close against him. He caught the faint sunny odor of her hair. "Why, dear lord?" she whispered. "We've slept side by side in the glens."

"Yes," he muttered. "But I don't trust myself any more."

She clapped her hands together. "Oh, good!"

"I—I——Hellfire! Two rooms, I said!"

The landlord shrugged. When he thought no one was looking, he was seen to tap his forehead.

The chambers were small, with no more furniture than a pallet, but seemed clean enough. Holger wondered how he would pay. He'd had too much else on his mind to remember he was broke. And Alianora, the woods child, might have forgotten about that aspect. Furthermore, gossip of his original entry would have spread through the town; someone would be sure to deduce that the dark-complexioned knight had gotten his face from Martinus, and perhaps that talk would reach the Saracen's ears. Well, he'd just have to cross his bridges as he came to them.

He shed his armor and donned his best tunic and hose, but kept his sword by him. When he emerged, he met Alianora. He was rather glad the corridor was too dark for her to see his expression. "Shall we go eat?" he asked lamely.

"Aye." Her words were a little choked. Suddenly she caught his hands. "Holger, what is 't ye dinna like about me?"

"Nothing," he said. "I like you very much."

"But that I be a swan-may, wild and unchristened? I could change that," she gulped. "I could learn to be a lady."

"I—Alianora—— You know I've got to get home. In spite of what they say, I've no real place in this world. So sometime I'll be leaving you. Forever. It'd be hard on both of us if . . . if I took your heart with me, and you kept mine here."

"But if ye canna get back?" she whispered. "If ye have to stay here?"

"That w-would be another story."

"How I hope ye fail! And yet I shall strive wi' all my micht to aid ye home, sith 'tis your wish." She turned from him, he could barely see how her head drooped. "Och, life is an unco thing."

He took her hand and they went downstairs.

The taproom was long and low, lighted by candles and a genuine fireplace. In these troubled times the landlord was only setting dishes on the table for one guest besides Holger and Alianora. As they entered, the man sprang from his bench with a shout. "*Ozh*——" He broke off when the Dane came into the light.

"I mistook you, fair sir," he bowed. "I thought you one whom I seek. Pray pardon, my lady and lord."

Holger studied him. This must be the Saracen. He was medium tall, slim and supple, elegant in flowing white shirt and trousers and in curly red shoes. A scimitar hung at his sashed waist. Under a turban with an emerald brooch and ostrich plume, his face was dark and narrow, eagle-nosed, sporting a pointed black beard and gold rings in his ears. He moved with feline smoothness and his tones were low and cultured, but Holger felt he'd be a nasty customer in a fight.

"Peace on you," said the Dane, trying to be polite. "May I present the Lady Alianora de la Forêt? I hight, umm, Sir Rupert of Graustark."

"I fear me I never heard of your demesne, good sir, but then I am from the far southwest and ignorant of these parts. Sir Carahue, onetime king of Mauretania, humbly at your service." The Saracen bowed almost to the ground. "Will you sup with me? 'Twould pleasure me to, ah——"

"Thank you, gracious knight," said Holger at once. It was a relief to have someone else pick up the dinner check. He and Alianora seated themselves. Carahue was a bit astonished at the girl's unconventional costume, but looked delicately away.

He insisted on having samples brought of the landlord's wines, sipped each, winced, and laid out the best accompaniment he could for each course. Holger could not resist saying, "I thought your religion banned strong drink."

"Ah, you mistake me, Sir Rupert. I am a Christian like yourself. Once, true, I fought for the paynim, but the gentle and chivalrous knight who overcame me also won me to the true Faith. Though even were I still a follower of Mahound, I would not be so discourteous as not to drink to your most beautiful lady's health."

They had a friendly supper, chatting of inconsequentials. Afterward Alianora yawned and went to bed, the close air made her sleepy. Holger and Carahue were still wakeful and settled down to some serious guzzling. The Dane demurred at first; he didn't like to be carried in every round. But the Saracen insisted on treating.

"I joy in the company of gentlefolk who can turn a sestina as well as break a lance," he declared, "and such are rare in this uncouth borderland. I beg you, let me express my gratitude."

"This is certainly no good place to go knocking about in," said Holger. Probingly he added, "Some great purpose must have brought you here."

"Yes, I seek a man." Carahue's eyes were shrewd above the rim of his goblet. "Mayhap you've heard news of him? A big fellow, about your size, but yellow-haired. Most likely he'll ride a black stallion and bear arms either of an eagle, sable on argent, or of three hearts sanguine and three lions passant or."

"Hmmm." Holger rubbed his chin and tried hard to appear calm. "I think I've heard something, but can't quite remember. What did you say his name was?"

"I didn't," said Carahue. "Let his name be what it will, if you will indulge me in such a whim. Truth is, he has many powerful enemies, who'd be swift to fall on him did word get abroad."

"Then you are a friend of his, sir?"

"Perhaps," said Carahue gently, "it were best that my own reasons be hid too. 'Tis not that I distrust you, Sir Rupert, but there are ears everyplace, some not human. And I am a stranger, not only to this part of the world, but to this whole time."

"What?"

Carahue watched Holger steadily, as if to catch any flicker of reaction, while he said, "This much I dare relate. I knew the man whom I seek centuries ago. But he vanished into realms unknown. I've learned that he came back once, when *le beau pays de France* stood in danger, and routed the heathen invaders, then vanished again. But that was after my time. For when he had first gone, I fared out to sea in quest of him. A great storm cast me ashore in Huy Braseal, where I was received in her enchanted castle by a most fair damsel." He sighed dreamily. "Time flowed strange in that realm, as 'tis said to do in Avalon or under Elf Hill. It seemed but a year to me that I abode with her; yet hundreds of years fled in the lands of men. When at last I got rumors of hosting throughout the Middle World, I stole the use of my lady-love's arts magical and learned that the whirlwind would first break in these eastern lands. I learned too that O——this knight whom I would fain meet again, would be drawn back by force of that gathering storm, from strange realms to which he had been exiled. So I helped myself to an enchanted ship, which bore me in a night from Huy Braseal to the south coast of this realm. There I got a horse and wandered north in search of him. But so far God has not willed that I succeed."

Carahue leaned back and drank thirstily. Holger scowled. By now he was quite prepared to believe such a tale. He'd experienced worse whoppers himself. But the Saracen could be lying . . . no, Holger had a notion he was telling the truth, as far as he went. The lean brown face was familiar. Somewhere, sometime, he must indeed have known Carahue. But as friend or foe? The other had carefully avoided committing himself on that point, and Holger didn't feel it would be wise to ask. True, the Moor had spoken well of the man he sought, but that didn't prove anything. Under the fantastic code of chivalry, men could sing each other's praises while carving out each other's livers.

The part about an acquaintance hundreds of years old was not unduly disturbing to Holger. He couldn't feel more alone and homesick than he already did. And the idea explained some things. He, Holger, of three hearts and three lions, had been a knight whom Morgan enticed to her timeless isle of Avàlon. Once he returned, when France needed him. She'd let him do so, probably not caring who won that war, and he'd gone back to her when it was over. Now again—— But this time his return was from a farther place, and Morgan opposed him with all her obscure powers.

"I would not seem overly meddlesome, Sir Rupert," said Carahue urbanely, "yet passing strange 'tis that you too should be questing along this uneasy bourne. Pray tell me, where lies your Graustark?"

"Oh, somewhat south," mumbled Holger. "I made a . . . a vow. The swan maiden kindly agreed to help me fulfill it."

Carahue arched his brows. Plainly, he didn't believe a word of that. But he merely smiled. "Come, shall we take pleasance with a song or two? Perchance you know a ballade, villanelle, or sirvente which would fall sweetly on ears too long accustomed to howling wolves and rainy winds."

"We can try," said Holger, glad to change the subject.

They traded songs for some hours. This required plenty of wine, to moisten the throat and lubricate the brain. Carahue was delighted with a rough translation of "Auld Lang Syne." He and Holger woke the household singing it when they helped each other, somewhat unsteadily, up the stairs and to bed.

17

HOLGER'S HEAD THUMPED next noon when he made his way to Martinus' shop, and Alianora was considerably silent. They left Hugi and the horses at the inn, for the landlord had been giving them suspicious looks. He had probably had experience with guests who were long on nobility and short on cash.

The wizard beamed at them. "Ah, I think you've looked into the flowing bowl once too often, my young friend," he chuckled, in the offensively patronizing manner of those who have not. "Eh, eh, boys will be boys, hey, my girl?" He picked up a bottle. "Now as it happens, I have here a very good and reasonably priced specific for bilious humours, bunions, rheums, leprosy, agues, plagues, and hangovers. Just toss down this tumblerful. . . . There, that wasn't so bad, was it?"

The pick-me-up did, indeed, remove Holger's pangs on the instant. He thought that if only he could get the formula and it worked in his universe, his fortune was made. But Martinus had turned grave again. The small man paced the shop with his hands behind his back, stared at the floor, and said low:

"I could not learn your identity, Sir Holger. A geas has been laid on every being which might have told me. That suggests you are indeed someone of importance. The enemy did not think of everything, however. I raised the fleet spirits of air, even called in Ariel as consultant, and they were still able to find where Cortana lies buried. The place is not overly far from here. But it's no trip I'd like to make."

Holger's heart thuttered. "Where?"

Martinus glanced at Alianora. "Do you know the church of St. Grimmin's-in-the-Wold?" he asked.

She bit her lip. "I ha' heard tell o' 't," she admitted.

"Well, that's where the sword is," said Martinus. "I imagine the Middle Worlders choose a site here in the east to get it far from its rightful owner, and St. Grimmin's specifically to make his quest hard should he ever get on its track." He shook his bald head. "I can't honestly recommend you go there, young fellow."

"What is this place?" asked Holger.

"An old abandoned church in the uplands north of here. Centuries ago it was raised as a mission, in the hope of converting the savage tribesmen thereabouts, and for a while it did have a congregation. Then a raiding chief murdered them all and the church has been in ruins ever since. They say the chief defiled the altar with a human sacrifice, so the building is no longer holy, but has become the biding place of evil spirits and bad luck. Not even the savages go near St. Grimmin's any more."

"Hm." Holger looked at his feet. He felt as if a weight lay on him. Martinus wasn't kidding.

For a moment he wondered why he should bother. Why should he even want to return home? What was there that drew him? Oh, yes, friends, memories, well-loved scenes, but to be completely honest, no one and nothing he would miss beyond endurance. War, hunger, drabness, depersonalization. Why, if he did succeed in returning, he might find himself at the same instant of space-time as he'd left. The conservation laws of physics suggested he would. And he and his fellows had been pinned down on a beach, knowing they were to die, hoping with a rapidly fading hope that they could stay alive just long enough for that one boat to reach the Swedish shore.

Hell, everything pointed to the other world's not even being his own. He belonged here, in this Carolingian universe; the other had been a place of exile. In so many ways this was a better and cleaner abode—— No, said his stubborn truthfulness, that wasn't fair. This cosmos had its own drawbacks. But simply by virtue of being different, didn't it promise him more adventure and opportunity than the best of the other earth?

A sunbeam straggling in a window touched Alianora's locks with fire. He'd never known a girl like her. If he chucked this whole stupid quest and went off with her, he could just about write his own ticket. King of the woods, or he could doubtless carve himself a realm in these turbulent borderlands, or if he wanted high civilization he could go with her to the Empire and——

And what? Chaos was still readying for battle. He thought of Alianora's idea that the Pharisees might draw their own twilight across the whole planet. He remembered what Morgan had mentioned about heedless play with worlds and suns, about men and their homes and hopes engulfed in destruction.

No, he really had no choice. No honorable man did, in such a time. He must do his best to get Cortana and give the weapon back to its rightful owner, or wield it himself if he was the one. Afterward, if there was an afterward, he could decide whether to continue attempting a return across the universes.

He looked up. "I'll go," he said.

"We will," corrected Alianora.

"As you wish," said Martinus gently. "And I pray for your fortune, Sir Holger. God be with you, God be with you, for I think you ride on behalf of us all."

He wiped his eyes with his sleeve. Then he donned a smile, rubbed his hands, and said, "Well, so much for that. Now about the bill, since you are bound on a perilous journey, I trust you wish to settle such matters at once?"

"Um, uh," said Holger.

"We've no the brass now," said Alianora. "But if ye'll send the score later, I'll see 'tis paid."

"I'd say you have plenty of brass," Martinus bridled. "See here, this shop does not give credit and——"

"But your sign says you can conjure up ever-filled purses," Holger began.

"Advertising," Martinus admitted. "Corroborative detail intended to lend artistic verisimilitude."

"Oh, come, dear old friend." Alianora smiled and took the magician's hand. "Ye'd no dun the man who's about to save the whole world, would ye? Why, your runes be your own share in the great emprise. They'll sing your name for aye."

"That won't pay *my* creditors," protested Martinus.

"Ah, but is 't no true that a noble deed is worth many riches?" Alianora stroked his cheek.

"Well," faltered Martinus, "there are words to that effect in Scripture, but——"

"Oh, my friend, thank ye! I knew ye'd agree! Thank ye!"

"But," bleated Martinus. "But you can't—I won't allow——"

"Nay, nay, no another word from ye. I wouldna dream o' taking more help than ye've already gi'en. Farewell, sweet man." Alianora kissed him roundly and, before he could recover, hustled Holger out of the shop.

Women! thought the Dane.

When they got back to the inn, they found Carahue lounging in the courtyard. He rose and bowed. "Your dwarfish companion intimated you would soon resume your travels, mademoiselle and Sir Rupert," he said.

"Yes," said Holger. He caught the landlord's fishy glance and added, "Maybe."

Carahue stroked his beard with a slim bejeweled hand. "Might I make bold to ask which way you fare?"

"North, I guess."

"Into the wilds? Truly a memorable adventure, if anyone survive to remember."

"I told you I've made a vow," grunted Holger.

"Pray pardon, friend," said Carahue. " 'Twould be discourteous to ask further when you are reluctant to speak. Yet may I offer some counsel? If you wish to preserve the secret of your goal, leave not quite so much room for speculation. Tongues will wag more when no firm facts bind them. Thus, some folk will guess you intend a knightly exploit like slaying one of the trolls which infest yonder uplands, often—as I've heard—stealing humans to eat; though the local people with whom I've chatted maintain such trolls are unkillable. Then again, other folk will insist that Sir Rupert went to beard the king of the heathen. But the peasant mind being what 'tis, most will believe you seek a treasure of gold buried somewhere there. And yet, how reconcile any of these objectives with the young lady's accompaniment of you? So folk will gab in idle hours, and the tale will spread like wildfire. If you'd hush the gossip, you must give a solid reason, preferably such an uncanny one that people would liefer not mention the affair."

Alianora fell for the line and blurted, "Och, 'tis a kittle enough journey, to the damned kirk o' St. Grimmin's."

Holger covered as best he might, "I swore a pilgrimage thither, in hopes of, uh, recovering what churchly vessels might remain. I, uh, I'd rather not speak about it because, uh, the reason for the penance is one I'd rather not speak about."

"Ah, so. Forgive me." The Saracen's gaze rested inscrutably on Holger. "Do you know, that's one part where I never thought to carry my own search? It seemed unlikely my man would appear there, when he returned. Yet now you make me wonder if indeed he might not. Besides, if I could help in a virtuous enterprise, my credit in Heaven would perchance rise above its present woeful level. Good company shortens the miles, to say naught of making them less dangerous. Perhaps we could travel together?"

Alianora traded a look with Holger. *You know him*, said her eyes. *You must decide.*

He hesitated. "There are more than bodily dangers," he said. "I think we may encounter black magic."

Carahue waved a negligent hand. "Your sword is straight and mine is curved." He smiled. "So between them they should fit any shape of foe."

Holger tugged his chin. He could certainly use another man. At the same time he knew Carahue must have reasons for dealing himself in.

Could he be an agent of Chaos? That was possible, but Holger's half-memories, which he was coming more and more to trust, said otherwise. He put himself in the Moor's place: out hunting an important man for some important purpose, failing, and then encountering another knightly vagabond with a rather thin story. Yes, memory said Carahue had that kind of mind, a curiosity which darted everywhere. Besides, he might well have guessed that Sir Rupert of Graustark had some connection with the person he himself sought: might perhaps know where that person was. Even if that turned out to be wrong, the uplands were worth a search. In every event Carahue had sound motives to string along with Sir Rupert.

"I very much wish the favor of your company," urged the Saracen. "Still more, of course, the favor of yours, most charming damsel. So much do I wish this that if you will agree of your great kindness, I shall insist on your being my guests as from last night. . . . No, no, protest not, I'll hear of nothing less."

Holger and Alianora gave him a look which he returned blandly. He must be pretty damn sure they were broke, and laughing up his flowing sleeve. Still, the prospect of leaving Tarnberg without having to fight the landlord was well-nigh irresistible.

"Done!" Holger stuck out his hand. Carahue grasped it. "Shall we swear comradeship?"

"Aye. Upon my knightly honor."

"And upon mine." Holger felt his decision had been good. Carahue would probably abide by the oath while the trip lasted; and once he, Holger, had Cortana in his hands, the Saracen would hardly be a menace. He said impulsively, "Bare is brotherless back."

Carahue started. "Where did you learn that?" he snapped.

"Why, well, it just came to me. Why do you ask?"

"I knew a man once who used that saying. The man I seek, if truth be told." Carahue's eyes lay keenly on them for a moment before he turned. "Well, let's dine and then make ready to depart. I think tomorrow dawn were best for that, eh?"

He was entertaining company at lunch, with jokes and songs and somewhat risqué reminiscences. Afterward he and Holger checked what equipment they had. His armor was a steel corselet, flaring at the shoulders and elaborately arabesqued; a spiked helmet with chainmail earflaps; greaves atop boots of tooled leather. His shield bore a six-pointed star argent on a field azure, border gules fleury or; his weapons included a bow and arrows; he rode a slim white mare. Alianora's dun gelding he declared to be good horseflesh, but added they had better acquire a mule, on which Hugi could ride with ample food supplies. He spent most of the afternoon talking down the prices of these items.

They went early to bed, but Holger lay awake for an hour. Despite every precaution, he knew Morgan le Fay would learn where he was bound, if she didn't already know—and would do something about it.

18

FOR TWO NIGHTS they stayed with peasants. Holger, who was not quick enough in the tongue to invent plausible details on the spot, must say as little as possible lest he betray himself to Carahue. The Saracen made conversation enough for both, sprightly, gallant, and aimed increasingly at the girl. This drove Holger still deeper into glum silence. He tried to push down his jealousy—what claim did he have on her?—but it bounced right back.

The third day they left roads and fields and houses behind them. That night they stayed in the hut of a shepherd, who told some grisly tales about savage raiders, worse ones about the trolls who sometimes ventured this far toward the valley. His was the last human habitation on their route, except for the cannibal villages.

Again they climbed mountains, steeper and higher than those to the east. Alianora said they were in the foothills of the titanic Jötun range. "And beyond is nobbut cold and dark and ice, lit by northern lights, for 'tis the home o' the giants."

Their goal was not quite that far, on a plateau short of the ultimate heights. But it was at least a week's journey, through a land harsh enough.

They rode between glacier-scarred boulders and wind-gnawed crags, up and up the long slopes, over razorback ridges and through ravines so narrow they were almost lightless. The woods thinned out into rare clumps of twisted scrub oak; grass grew sparse and stiff; the air was chilly by day and cold by night, with clouds scudding over the pale sun and the bitterly brilliant stars. Often they had to ford streams that torrented from the peaks. It was all their animals could do not to be yanked away to drowning. Hugi, whose short legs hardly came below the packs on which he rode, was the only one who didn't get drenched. He would shout jovial remarks like "Ship ahoy!" and "Stow the miz- zenmast!" which got little appreciation. Carahue snuffed and sneezed and swore imaginatively at the weather (he denied that this land had climate), but he stuck with the others.

"When I get home," he said, "I shall lie under orange blossoms in the sun. Slave girls will play me music and drop grapes in my mouth. To keep fit, I shall take exercises: twice daily will I twiddle my fingers. After a few months I will weary of this and set forth on a new knightly quest: let us say, as far as the nearest coffee shop."

"Coffee," sighed Holger. He was even running low on Unrich's tobacco, or whatever the stuff was.

Alianora turned swan from time to time and flew ahead to check their course. When she was gone from view, the fourth day in the wil- derness, Carahue regarded Holger with unaccustomed sobriety. "Despite her taste in clothes," he said, "that is a girl whose like is rarely found."

"I know," nodded Holger.

"Forgive my impudence in asking, but God did give me eyes to see with. She's not your leman, is she?"

"No."

"The more fool you."

Holger couldn't quite resent that. It was probably correct.

" 'Tis wha' I ha' been telling him and telling him and telling him," rumbled Hugi. "Yon knichts be an eldritch breed. They'll cross the world to rescue a maiden, and then dinna know aught to do wi' her but take her home and mayhap beg a bit o' hair ribbon to wear on their sleeve. 'Tis a wonder their sort ha' no died oot erenoo."

Alianora came back toward dusk. "I've seen the kirk from afar," she reported. "I saw also, closer to us, two strongholds o' the wild men, wi' skulls on poles all around, and the folk in a bustle as if readying for war."

"They are." Holger nodded.

Alianora frowned. "I've scouted a way for us through one pass, up onto the wold. No settlements lie near, belike because a troll dwells in some cave thereabouts. Yet the widely ranging huntsmen may spy us e'en so, and bring a party to capture us for our flesh."

"Ha, a sad end to a valiant knight, barbecued in his own armor," said Carahue. He grinned. "Though methinks Sir Rupert and Hugi and I would prove tough steaks, nothing like your tender pretty limbs."

Alianora smiled in a confused way and blushed. Carahue took her hand. "Come worst to worst," he said gravely, "you must fly and not heed us. The world can well spare our sort, but would become dreary indeed without you to light it."

She shook her head, tongue-tied, and did not quickly withdraw her hand. *This boy*, thought Holger, *is an operator*. He couldn't find any words of his own, and couldn't stand to listen. So he rode ahead, his mood thickening by the hour. Carahue was not poaching, he told himself; but himself paid scant attention. Didn't the guy have any sense of decency or whatever? Didn't Alianora have any sense, question mark? . . . Well, how could she? She'd never been exposed to this sort of thing before. She'd take the most worn-out flatteries for wit and honest sentiments. Blast his soul, Carahue had no right to shoot a sitting swan like that. Besides, on a trip as dangerous and important as this, no one had a right to—to—— Oh, damn it all, anyway!

At evening they found themselves in a slight dip. Ahead bulked the slopes they must climb tomorrow, rock piled on rock till a distant ridge stood back and saw-toothed against the sky. But in this dale a cataract foamed over a slate-blue cliff, into a lake tinged red with sundown. Closer at hand, the shore was low and still. A flock of wild ducks clattered off as the humans neared, to settle near the opposite bank, a mile away. The hush returned.

"I hoped we could reach this loch," said Alianora. "If we leave some fishlines out o'ernicht, we can make a better breakfast than salt pork and hardtack."

Hugi shook his big shaggy head. "I know na, lassie. This whole land smells evil, but here's a stench I ne'er met."

Holger inhaled a breeze tinged with damp green odors. "Seems okay to me," he said. "Anyway, we can't get around the lake before nightfall."

"We could go back uphill and camp above," said Carahue.

"Retrace our steps two miles?" Holger sneered. "Do so if you wish, sir. But I'm not afraid to sleep here."

The Saracen flushed and bit back an angry retort. Alianora hurried to break the silence by exclaiming, "See, yon's a good dry spot."

Moss squelched underfoot, soaked as a sponge. But a great rock heaved above, the slant side spotted by lichen, the flat top covered with soil that bore short thick grass. A dead shrub near the middle offered ready-made fuel. Alianora spread her arms and said, "Why, 'tis as if prepared for us."

"Aye, so 'tis," grumbled Hugi. No one heeded. He must chop wood with a hatchet from the pack mule, while the men established a protective circle and took care of the animals. The sun slipped down under western heights but that half of the sky remained crimson, as if a fire had been lit by giants.

Alianora jumped up from the blaze she herself had kindled. "Whilst a good bed o' coals gets started," she said, "I'll go set our hooks."

"No, remain here, I beg you," said Carahue. He sat cross-legged, his handsome dark visage turned merrily up to her. Somehow, through their hard traveling, he had kept his picturesque clothes nearly immaculate.

"But would ye no like a mess o' fresh fish?"

"Aye, certes. However, 'tis worthless compared to one hour more, of this too short life, in the presence of utter beauty."

The girl turned her head. Holger saw how the blush stained her face and bosom. Still more acutely was he aware of her young curves within the swan tunic, of great gray eyes and soft lips and fluttering hands. "Nay," she whispered. "I dinna know what ye means, Sir Carahue."

"Sit down, and I shall do my poor best to explain." He patted the turf beside him.

"Why . . . why——" She threw Holger a blurred look. He snapped his teeth together and turned his back. From the edge of an eye he saw her join the other man. The Saracen murmured:

" 'Tis honorable that an errant knight
go boldly forth however dim the chances,
and not alone upon such times as lances
gleam high and then are shattered in the fight:
for when the golden daystar burns less bright
than one pure hope at which his heartbeat dances,
'tis honorable that an errant knight
go boldly forth however dim the chances.
And so, since your rare loneliness has quite
ensnared my soul with one or two sweet glances,
I dare ask more than lordship of ten Frances—
that you a moment linger in my sight;
'tis honorable that an errant knight
go boldly forth however dim the chances."

"Oh," stammered Alianora, "I, I, I canna think what to say."

"You need not say, fairest of damsels," he answered. "Only be."

"I'll set the lines," Holger barked. He snatched them up and scrambled down off the rock. His neck ached with the effort of not looking back.

By the time he was out of sight among the reeds, his shoes and hose were wet. A fat lot she'd care if he caught pneumonia. *Now cut that self-pity out!* If Alianora tumbled for such a slicker, Holger had none but himself to blame. He'd been given first refusal, hadn't he? Only, under the circumstances he'd had to refuse. What a lousy trick to play on a man.

He slashed at the plants with his knife. Except for the dagger belt, he was unarmed, having doffed his heavy mail on making camp. So had Carahue; but Holger lacked the Saracen's gift of elegance, he was muddy and sweaty and rumpled. He didn't even wear his own face any more. No wonder Alianora——Well, what did she matter to him? He ought to be glad if she found someone who'd take her off his hands. Goddam bulrushes!

He emerged on the water's edge. Very still it lay under the black cliffs, the purple eastern sky where a moon and one star hung, the sullen red to the west. The surface was touched by that sunset light as if with blood, but in so thin a shimmer that he could sense the darkness below. The reeds shivered and rustled; Holger's footsteps plashed startlingly loud. Frogs leaped from an old log that had drifted into the bank. He spread his lines out on this and started to bait the hooks with meat scraps.

The cold enveloped him, ate inward and made him shake. His fingers were clumsy, he must squint through the failing light to see a hook. *And I could be on Avalon this minute,* he thought. *Or even, by hell, under Elf Hill with Meriven. Doesn't that hillbilly swan wench know what she's doing to me, parading around half naked? Satan take all women, anyway. They've got exactly one purpose in the world. Judas, but Meriven sure served that purpose.*

His hand slipped. The hook went into his finger. He pulled it out with a blasphemous oath, drew his steel dagger and stabbed the log because he must stab something.

Laughter rang like the cataract. He flung his head around and glimpsed the white shape risen behind him. Then his wrists were pinned at his back. An arm clamped about his neck. He felt himself heaved backward and down. The lake closed over him.

19

THROTTLED, HE TRIED to kick, but the faintness was already upon him. His brain spun toward night. When he was let go, sheer reflex opened his mouth in a gasp.

He did not drown. He sat up. For a moment he couldn't think who he was, or why or where. Awareness returned. But he needed minutes to see what lay about, for his eyes were not trained to such things.

He sat on white sand that reached beyond sight in graceful ripple marks. Here and there lay stones covered with a brilliant green overgrowth of algae, whose long filaments wavered upward. A luminosity filled the air, akin to the sourceless un-light in Faerie, but faintly greenish. Only . . . not air. For bubbles streamed from his mouth and nostrils, to rise like tiny polished moons. He saw a fish go by, from the wanness on his left to the perspectiveless distances on his right. He sprang to his feet, bounced, and drifted down with ghostly slowness. His body seemed to be without weight. The water flowed sensuously around each movement.

"Welcome, Sir 'Olger." The voice was cold and sweet.

He turned. A woman poised lazily before him. She was nude and paper white, with delicate green traces of veins under the skin. Long hair floated about her shoulders, fine and green as the algal weeds. Her face was broad and flat-nosed, with yellow eyes and a heavy sensuous mouth. Neck, torso, limbs, and hands were by contrast not quite human in their slenderness. Holger had never seen such grace as was hers, save in eels.

"Who, who, who?" he choked.

"Nay, now," she laughed, "you are no owl, but a highborn knight. Welcome, I say." She edged closer with a kick. He saw her feet were mostly toe, and webbed. Lips and nails were pale green. But the sight was not horrible. On the contrary! Holger had to remind himself he was in serious trouble.

"Forgive my impetuous invitation." Bubbles swarmed bright from her mouth. Some clustered like jewels in her tresses. "I must needs seize the fleeting moment when you had no iron and were in an unblessed mood. Truly, no harm was meant you."

"Where the devil am I?" he exploded.

"Beneath the lake where I, its nixie, have dwelt these many lonely centuries." She took his hands. Her own were soft and cool, with an underlying sense of the strength that had captured him. "Fear not. My spell guards you from drowning."

Holger noticed his breath. It felt no different from usual, except for a slight heaviness on his chest. He rolled his tongue around in his mouth and squirted saliva between his teeth. Somehow, he thought—striving for a toehold on sanity—the forces called magical must be extracting oxygen from the water for him and forcing it into a thin protective layer, perhaps monomolecular, on his face. The rest of him was in direct contact with the lake. His clothes flopped soggy. Yet he was warm enough. . . . *What am I gabbling about? I've got to get out of here!*

He jerked free of her. "Who put you up to this?" he demanded.

She stretched her arms over her head till the verdant hair entwined their whiteness, arched her back, and poised on tiptoe. "None," she smiled. "You cannot imagine how wearisome existence grows, alone and immortal. When a beautiful young warrior, with locks like the sun and eyes like heaven, chanced hither, I must love him on the instant."

His cheeks burned. The detached part of him reflected that she, being of the Middle World, was as immune to the illusion which disguised him as he was himself. Even so . . . how did she know his name? "Morgan le Fay!" he flung out.

"What matter?" Her shrug was a flow along her whole body. "Come, my house lies near. A feast awaits you. Afterward——" She swayed close. Her eyelids drooped.

"This is no accident," he insisted. "I expected Morgan would track us. When we passed by this lake, she arranged everything. I don't believe my own actions were free, even."

"Oh, fear not that. No mortal of good character can be touched by enchantment, unless he himself wishes."

"Well, I know what my character was like at the time, and I suspect I was prodded into the right frame of mind, if not forced. Very well. Begone, you!" Holger drew the sign of the cross.

The nixie smiled her slumbrous smile. She shook her head, a slow weaving back and forth with billows running through the loose hair. "Nay, too late. While you are here, whither your own desires have brought you, you may not escape so cheaply. Aye, why should I not own the truth, that her majesty of Avalon commanded me to lurk by the shore and abide my opportunity? I am to keep you here until she sends for you, which will be after the war that is almost begun." She drifted upward till she lay horizontally before his face. Her thin wire-strong fingers reached out to stroke his hair. "Yet 'tis also truth, how glad of your questing Rusel is, and how cunningly she will strive to make your stay joyous."

Holger wrenched away and kicked against the sand. He shot up. His limbs caught the water and he swam toward the unseen surface. The nixie glided alongside, effortlessly, still smiling. She didn't oppose him herself, but beckoned.

Lean shapes hurtled into sight. Jaws snapped before Holger's nose. He looked into the blank eyes and needle-toothed beak of the biggest pike he had ever seen. Others closed in, a dozen, a hundred. One ripped his hand. Pain jabbed; his blood came out like red smoke. He stopped. The pike circled on every side. Rusel made another gesture. They swam off, but slowly, and remained on the edge of vision.

Holger bobbed back down to the sand. He needed a few minutes to get his breath and pulse under control.

The nixie took his hand and kissed the wound. It closed as if it had never been made. "Nay, you must stay, Sir 'Olger," she purred. " 'Twould be a deadly disappointment for me did you seek so discourteously to leave."

"Deadlier for me," he managed to say.

She laughed and took his arm. "Far too soon will Queen Morgan claim you. Meanwhile, come, consider yourself a prisoner of war, honorably taken in an honorable captivity. Which I shall seek to lighten for you."

"But my friends——"

"Fear not, my sweeting. By themselves they're no menace to the great purpose. They can be suffered to return home unscathed." With a flick of malice: "From a distance, after the sun that is fatal to me had sunk, I espied certain attitudes struck in yonder camp. Meseems the swan maiden will soon let herself be consoled for you. If not this very eventide, then surely within a sennight."

Holger clenched his fists. He felt strangled. That worthless Saracen——

But Alianora had fallen all over herself to heed Carahue's flatteries. The little bird-brain!

Rusel laid one hand on Holger's neck. Her lips were close to his. He saw how they swelled. "All right," he said thickly. "Let's go to your house, at least."

"How you gladden me, gallant sir! You shall see what dainties have been prepared. And what pleasures undreamed of by the oafish land dwellers there may be in these depths, where no weight hinders the freedom of the body."

Holger could well imagine. If he was caught, why not enjoy it? "Let's go," he repeated.

Rusel fluttered her lashes. "Will you not first remove that ugly sack?"

He looked at his water-logged garments and back at her. His hands fell to his belt.

But instead he clapped hold on Duke Alfric's dagger. Memory flashed in him. For a moment he stood rigid. Then he shook his head, violently, and said, "Later, at the house. I expect I'll want them again sometime."

"Nay, Morgan will garb you in silk and vair. But let us not anticipate my sorrow when you must depart. Come!" The nixie arrowed off. Holger followed, threshing by comparison like a paddle-wheel steamer. She returned and laughed as she swam circles around him. Often she darted in to touch his mouth with her own, but slipped free before he could grab her. "Soon, soon," she promised. The pike trailed after. Their eyes were dull lanterns behind the jaws.

Rusel's house was not the coral palace he had half expected. Walls or roof were useless here. A ring of boulders bore weeds that streamed upward out of sight, forming curtains of green and brown which stirred, shifted, rippled. Fish darted in and out, minnows that fled at the nixie's approach and trout with iridescent scales that nuzzled her fingers. As he passed through the weeds, Holger felt their touch cool and slimy on his skin.

Beyond, partitions of the same sort marked off a few large rooms. Rusel conducted him to a feasting chamber. Here stood ghostly frail chairs woven of fish bones, around a stone table inset with shell and nacre, laid with covered dishes of gold.

"Observe, my lord," she said. "I've even gotten rare wines for you, by the help of Queen Morgan." She handed him a spherical vessel with a stoppered tube, not unlike a South American *bombilla*. "You must drink from this, lest the lake water spoil the contents. But do drink, to our better acquaintance."

Her own clinked against his. The wine was a noble vintage, full and heady. She leaned close. Her nostrils dilated, her lips invited him. "Welcome," she repeated. "Would you dine at once? Or shall we first——"

I can afford one night here, he thought. His temples hammered. *Of course I can. I've got to, even to disarm her suspicion before I try to make a break.* "I'm not very hungry at the moment," he said.

She made a purring noise and began to unlace his jerkin. He fumbled again with his own belt. As he took it off, her eye fell on the empty sheath and the filled one beside.

"But that can't be steel!" she exclaimed. "I'd have sensed the nearness of cold iron. Ah, I see."

She drew the blade and regarded it closely. "The Dagger of Burning," she spelled out. "Strange name. Faerie workmanship, not so?"

"Yes, I won it from Duke Alfric, when I overcame him in battle," Holger bragged.

"I'm not surprised, noble lord." She rubbed her head against his breast. "No other man could have done so; but you are no other man." Her attention wandered back to the dagger. "I've never seen that metal before," she said. "All I have down here is gold and silver. I keep trying to tell the barbarian priests I want bronze, but they are so stupid even when conscious, let alone in a prophetic trance, that it never occurs to them the demon of the lake might have use for something with a good cutting edge. I have a few flint knives left from ancient times when such were offered me, but they're worn down to nubbins."

Holger wanted to grab her, when she curved and floated beside him. He needed his entire will to say, with such overdone casualness he was sure she would pounce on it, "Well then, keep this blade as a souvenir of myself."

"I shall find many ways to thank you, bright lord," she promised. She was about to continue unlacing him, with fingers that kept playfully straying, when he took the dagger back and tested the edge with his thumb.

"Pretty dull at the moment," he said. "Let me ashore and I'll whet it for you."

"Oh, no!" Her smile turned predatory. She wasn't used to humans, wherefore his clumsy acting could fool her, but neither was she stupid. "Let's talk of more likely things."

"You can hold my feet, or tether me, or whatever," he said. "I do have to get into the air to sharpen this knife. Such metal requires the heat of a fire, you see."

She shook her head. With a wry grin, he relaxed. It had been a long shot anyway, and for the moment, with this supple creature beside him, he wasn't sorry to have failed. "As you wish," he said, dropped the knife and laid his hands on her flanks.

Perhaps his lack of insistence deceived her. Or perhaps, thought Holger, not without an inward exasperated curse, his destiny had too much momentum to end here. For she said, "I have a grindstone among my sacrifices. Will that not serve? I understand such a device will sharpen a blade."

He fought down a shiver. "Tomorrow."

She darted from his embrace. "Now, now," she said. Her eyes glistened. He had noticed that lunatic capriciousness in the Faerie folk too. "Come, you should see my treasures." She tugged his hand.

Reluctantly, he followed. The pike glided behind. His throat was almost too tight for speech, but he managed conversation: "Did you say the barbarians make you offerings?"

"Aye." Her laughter jeered. "Each spring they troop hither to do worship and cast into the lake that which they think will please me. Some does." She parted a living arras. "I bring the gifts here to my treasury. The foolish ones are always good for a jest, if naught else."

Holger was first aware of the bones. Rusel must have whiled away many hours arranging the parts of skeletons in artistic patterns. The skulls which studded that lattice had jewels in their eyesockets. Elsewhere were stacked cups, plates, ornaments, looted from civilized lands by the heathen or not unskillfully made by their own smiths. In one corner was a disordered heap of miscellaneous objects that must also have been considered valuable by the tribesmen (if they were not simply sloughing their white elephants off on the demon)—water-ruined books from some monastery, a crystal globe, a dragon's tooth, a broken statuette, a child's sodden rag doll at which Holger found his eyes stinging a little, and junk less identifiable after long immersion. The nixie burrowed into the pile with both arms.

"So they give you humans," said Holger, very softly.

"A youth and a maiden each year. I've really no use for them. I'm not a troll or a cannibal woman to enjoy such meat, but they seem to think so. And the sacrifices do wear the most beautiful costumes." Rusel threw him a glance over her shoulder, as innocent as the look of a cat. She had no soul.

With a surge of strength under the white skin she hauled the grindstone forth. The wooden framework appeared rotten and the bronze fittings were badly corroded; but the wheel did still respond to the crank. "Aren't my baubles pretty?" she asked, waving her hand around the room. "Choose what you wish. Anything, my lord, just so you include myself."

In spite of the bones, Holger must force his words: "Let's take care of the dagger first. Can you turn the wheel?"

"As fast as you like. Try me." Her look suggested he was welcome to try anything. But she planted her feet on the sand and whirled the crank till he felt a vortex in the water. More loud than through air, the drone entered his ears, and the whine as he laid the knife to the wheel.

The pike crowded close, their gaunt heads aimed at him.

"Faster," he said. "If you can."

"Aye!" Metal screamed. The frame vibrated; green flakes drifted from the bolts. *Christ, let this thing hold together long enough!*

The pike flicked themselves closer. Rusel was taking no chances while he held a weapon. Her pets could strip him of flesh in three minutes. Holger rallied what courage remained to him and narrowed his attention to the dagger. He didn't know if his scheme would work. But even here under the lake, the blade must be heating up, and he could see the fine cloud of metal dust grow thicker around its edge.

"Are you done?" panted Rusel. Her hair had plastered itself to shoulders and breasts and belly. The amber eyes smoldered at him.

"Not yet. Faster!" He leaned his mass against the knife.

The flare nearly blinded him. *Magnesium will burn in water.*

Rusel shrieked. Holger guarded his face with one hand and swung the knife at the fish. One of them slashed his calf. He kicked himself free, broke through the green curtains and upward.

The nixie circled beyond the blue-white glare, beyond the range of his own dazzled eyes. She yelled at her pike. One darted near. Holger waved the torch and it fled. Either the fish couldn't stand the ultraviolet themselves or—more likely—Rusel's influence over them was bounded by distance like all magic, and she couldn't get near enough to Holger to set the water wolves on him.

He kicked with his legs and clawed with his free hand. Would he never reach the top? As if across light-years he heard the nixie's tone change to softness. " 'Olger, 'Olger, would you leave me? You'll ride to your doom in a barren land. 'Olger, come back. You know not what pleasures we could have——"

He screwed his will power tight and plowed on. Her rage burst forth. "Die, then!" Suddenly he inhaled water. The spell was off him. He choked. His lungs seemed to catch fire. He almost dropped his magnesium torch. He saw Rusel dart near in a cloud of her pike. He thrust her back with the cruel light, closed his mouth and swam. Up, up, darkness roiled in his brain, strength drained from his muscles, but up.

He broke the surface, coughed, spat, and gulped his chest full of air. A gibbous moon touched the lake with broken light. He held the torch below while he floundered toward the gray shore. It burned out just as he waded into the reeds. He ran to get well inland before he collapsed.

The cold struck his wet clothes and went on through. He lay with clattering teeth and waited for enough energy to seek the camp. He didn't feel victorious. He'd won this round, but there would be others. And . . . and . . . oh, damn everything, why did he have to escape so soon?

20

AT LAST HE MADE his plashy way back. The stone lifted from the ground like a ship, black in the night, and those moon-tinged clouds that the wind whipped along behind it gave an illusion that the ship was under weigh. Through what seas? wondered Holger. The fire had burned to embers, a riding light the color of clotted blood. As he crawled up on top, he saw the horses bunched together in a shadowy mass that might have been a cabin amidships. Carahue stood at the prow, staring north. The wind that skirled as if through unseen shrouds flapped his cloak with cracking noises. Moonlight shimmered off his drawn saber.

A furious little form seized Holger at the waist and tried to shake him. "Mon, where've ye been the while?" cried Hugi. "We've been fretted sick o'er ye. Na word or track past the lake's edge, till ye return soaked and reeking o' wicked places. Wha' happened?"

Carahue half turned, so that Holger caught the gleam of an eye under the spiked helmet. But the Saracen's attention remained afar. Holger looked that way. The edge of this vale cut off view of the mountains beyond; he thought, though, he saw a dim wavering redness, as if a great fire burned somewhere there.

Fear struck him. "Where's Alianora?" he snapped.

"Gone in search of you, Sir Rupert," Carahue answered. His tone remained smooth. "When we could not trace you, she assumed swan guise to look from above. That blaze yonder had already been kindled, and I fear she went thither. There can be no good gathering around it, in this land."

"And you didn't stop her?" Rage drove the cold from Holger. He walked stiff-legged toward the Moor. "By God's bones——"

"Pray enlighten me, gentle knight," said Carahue in his most buttered voice. "How was I to stop her when she announced her intention and was airborne before I could seize her?" He sighed. "Such a seizable damsel, too."

"Ha' done," growled Hugi. "Tell us richt the noo where ye went . . . uh . . . Rupert." As Holger hesitated, the dwarf stamped his foot and added, "Aye, well I know somehoo the enemy's made a fool o' ye yet again. We maun hear how 'twas this time, that we may know what t' await."

The strength poured from Holger. He sat down, hugged his knees, and recited fully how he had been caught and had escaped. Hugi tugged his beard and muttered. "Och, so, so, aye, a tricksy nixie. I'm no ane to boast I tauld ye so, and thus I'll say no word about hoo I warned this were a bad spot for us. Remember the next time, and heed me. I'm more oft richt than wrong, as nobbut ma modesty forbids me to prove wi' many a tale oot o' ma past, like yon time when a manticore were lurking in the Grotto o' Gawyr and I tauld puir young Sir Turold and I tauld him——"

Carahue ignored the background noise to drawl, "Meseems the fulfillment of your vow has more than common importance, Sir Rupert, if the way is made this difficult."

Holger was too tired and discouraged to head off the Saracen's suspicion with a claim that everything had been mere coincidence. He removed his clothes and was looking about for a towel when a whirr overhead and a white flash made him break all records for the resuming of soggy pants.

Alianora landed and became human. She drew a gasp when she saw Holger, took a step toward him, and checked herself. He couldn't read her expression in the coal-glow; she was only a supple shadow edged with red. "So ye're safe," she greeted him, coolly enough. "Good. I o'erflew that encampment lighting up the sky, atop a bald peak, and got news." Her voice trailed off. She shuddered and turned toward Carahue as if seeking warmth. Teeth sparkled in his beard. He took his cloak off and threw it over her shoulders.

"What saw you, bravest as well as fairest of maidens?" he murmured, making rather more fuss than necessary about adjusting the garment on her.

"A coven was met." She stared past them, into the darkness that streamed and whimpered under the moon. "I've never seen the like erenow, but it must have been a coven. Thirteen men stood about the balefire that was kindled before a great altar stone where a crucifix big as life lay broken. Most o' the men were savage chiefs, to judge from their plumes and skin garb. A few must ha' flown hither from the south

. . . old they were, old, wi' sic evil writ on their faces in the firelicht
that the sight nigh blasted me from the air. Beyond the licht, where I
could scarce see them, waited creatures. Och, glad I am they were in
the darkness, for I fear that wha' little I saw will stand 'fore me in
dreams. Yet the coven watched the altar stone, where bled a———" She
gulped and must force the words out—"a wee babe, slaughtered like
any pig. And a blackness were forming atop the altar, taller nor a man.
. . . I turned and fled. That were an hour or more agone. Not e'en for
ye could I bring myself down again, 'twere no possible, ere the clean
winds had blown some o' the grue out o' me."

She sank to her knees and covered her face. Carahue stooped over
her, but she pushed him aside. Hugi's gnarled shape approached, laid
an arm over her back, and took her hand. She clung to the dwarf. The
breath hissed between her lips.

Carahue went to Holger and said grimly, "So 'tis true what I heard
in Huy Braseal and what has been rumored among men since my return.
Chaos arms for war."

He stood a while longer, silent among shadows, before he raised
his sword a trifle and said, "My last time on earth, hundreds of years
agone, I once wandered into these same marchlands. In those days the
hillmen were heathen too, but a clean sort of heathen. They did not
worship devils nor eat human flesh. They've been corrupted, to be the
instruments of man's enemy. Their chiefs have been received into the
coven, and the coven gives those chiefs orders to lead the tribesmen
against the valley folk. Mayhap this meeting tonight was the last of
many. The cannibals may start gathering their hosts tomorrow."

"I think so," Holger answered mechanically.

"You think much you do not choose to relate," Carahue said.

He thrust his blade into its sheath. "No matter. We need sleep worse
than we need talk. Another time I shall take up certain questions with
you."

"Thanks for the warning," said Holger.

He hadn't expected he could sleep at all, and certainly his slumber
was not restful, an uneasy half-consciousness crawling with visions. He
was glad when Hugi roused him to take his watch, gladder still when
day broke.

They bolted their rations, saddled their horses, and were off. Holger
did not look back at the lake, where it glimmered beneath white vapors,
and soon it was far behind. The weather had turned chill, a scud of gray
clouds under a leaden overcast. The mountain slopes up which the party
rode grew ever more barren, until nothing covered them but clumps of
harsh silvery grass. Pinnacles thrust eroded outlines across a horizon

dominated in the north by a sheer scarp. Alianora said they must climb this, through a gap she had spotted from the air, to get out on the wold. There were easier passes, but those lay too close to the savage towns. Nobody dwelt near this one.

Hugi wrinkled his nose and spat. "Aye, well micht they folk shun these parts," he rumbled. "Each step forward strengthens the troll stench. Yon cliff maun be riddled wi' his caves and burrows."

Holger stole a glance at Alianora's troubled face, where she rode between him and Carahue. "We've overcome quite a variety of creatures thus far," he said, hoping to cheer her. "Witches, Pharisees, a dragon, a giant, a werewolf. What's a troll among friends, except a Christmas song?"

"Eh?" Startled, she blinked at him.

"Sure." But he discovered that the Romance language would not render the English phrase: "Troll, the ancient Yuletide carol."

Hugi said dourly, "Methinks I'd liefer face all oor past playmates rolled into ane, than the haunter o' yon pass. Like a wolverine to a bear, so be a troll to a giant. Not so big, mayhap, but fierce beyond measure, cunning, and gripsome o' life. Many giants ha' been killed by mortal men, this way or that, but the tale is that no knicht ha' ever come off victor against a troll."

"So?" Carahue lifted his brows. "Are they not pained by iron?"

"Aye. That is, iron will burn 'em, as a red-hot poker 'ud burn ye. Yet ye micht easily overcome a man who fought ye wi' sic a weapon, and soon recover from what wounds ye got. Trolls are akin to the ghouls, and thus may gang near holiness if it be not too great. Yer cross will give scant help unless ye be a saint. More I dinna know, for few who saw a troll ha' e'er returned to describe habits nor habitat."

"It would be a famous exploit to slay one," said Carahue on a note of chivalrous ambition. *Me, I'll stay obscure if I may,* Holger thought.

They plodded on. It was near noon when they emerged from a rocky defile and spied the hillmen.

There was no warning. Holger reined in with a curse. His heart slammed against his ribs, once, before he lost fear in simple urgency. He stared ahead. Whetted, his eyes saw with the fullness of vision by lightning.

There were perhaps a score, dogtrotting from the north, down the mountainside. They swerved as they glimpsed him and approached quickly. Their cries were like dogs barking.

The leader was big and gaunt, his yellow hair and beard in twin braids, his face painted in red and blue stripes. A headdress of plumes and ox horns rose over him. His shoulders were covered by a mantle of badger skins, his midriff by a shaggy kilt. But he had a steel battle ax in his hand.

The others were similar. Axes, swords, spears gleamed among them. One wore the rusty tilting helmet of some murdered knight, a horrible faceless thing to see upon his naked body. Another blew a wooden whistle as he ran; the notes trilled between wolfish voices.

"Back!" exclaimed Carahue. "We'll have to flee!"

"We can't escape them," groaned Holger. "Men can run down horses. And we've got to reach St. Grimmin's soon."

A javelin clattered yards before him. "Get aloft Alianora!" he shouted.

"Nay," she said. One hand clutched blindly for his.

"You can fight better thus," said Carahue. Holger wished his own wits operated that quickly. The girl nodded, kicked loose from her stirrups, and transformed. The swan rose in a thunder of wings.

The war band stopped. A yell went up. Several covered their eyes. "*Allah akbar!*" exploded Carahue. "They're terrified of magic. Merciful saints, I meant to say."

The swan dove toward the savages. The leader shook his ax at her, snatched a bow from one of the men and nocked an arrow. The swan veered just in time. The leader shouted at his men, uncouth noises borne faintly down the wind to his quarry. He kicked those who had fallen prostrate until they climbed to their feet.

"Aye." Hugi's mouth tightened in the white beard. "That un be in the coven. He's seen worse witchcraft nor this. He's heartening the others to rush on against us."

"Their nerve is none too steady, though," said Carahue, lightly as if he sat at a banquet. He strung his own short double-curved bow. "Could we pull another trick or two——" He cocked an eye at Holger.

The Dane thought wildly of parlor tricks, of urging the cannibal chief to take a card, any card. . . . Wait! "Hugi," he gasped, "Strike me a light."

"What is't ye do?"

"Light! Damn your questions! Fast!"

The dwarf got flint and steel from his belt pouch while Holger stuffed his pipe. His fingers shook. By the time he had it lit, the hillmen were horribly close. He could see the scar on one cheek, the bone in another nose; he heard their bare feet slap the ground, almost he heard their breath. He inhaled, raggedly, to fill his mouth with smoke.

He exhaled.

The savages skidded to a halt. Holger fumed till his eyes smarted and his nose ran. God be praised, there was no wind just now. He guided

Papillon with his knees, raising his cloak behind his head with both hands, to provide a dark backdrop for the smoke. Slowly, he rode toward the warriors. They had stopped dead. He saw them waver. Their jaws were slack and their eyes a-bug.

Holger flapped his arms. "Boo!" he shouted.

One minute afterward, the heathen were out of sight. The slope was littered with weapons they had dropped. Their screams drifted from the ravine into which they had bolted. The leader held his place alone. Holger drew sword. The leader snarled and ran too. Carahue shot an arrow after him, but missed.

Alianora landed, became a girl, threw herself against the Dane and hugged his leg. "Oh, Holger, Holger," she choked. Carahue dropped his bow to clutch his sides, for the echoes had begun to ring with his laughter.

"Genius!" he whooped. "Sheer genius! Rupert, I love you for this!"

Holger smiled shakily. He'd simply taken another crib from literature—the *Connecticut Yankee*—but there was no reason to discuss that point. Enough that it had worked.

"Let's get going," he said. "Their boss may yet whip some courage back into them."

Alianora sprang to the saddle. Her cheeks were flushed, and she looked happier than she had for some time. Hugi observed grumpily, "Aye, their guts oozed oot fast enough. Yet 'twas ne'er said yon breed are aught but bonny fighters. Why should they shy from a seeming touch o' wizardry? Because o' late they've seen so much o' 't, and so nasty, that their nerves are close to breaking. That's all. We've no seen the last o' them."

Holger had to agree. He doubted the band had intercepted him coincidentally. Morgan must have ordered it out—even across the feared pass—the moment she learned Rusel had not been able to keep him prisoner. She wouldn't quit after this failure, either.

Carahue edged his mount close. "Methought I heard the fair lady call you by a name strange to me," he remarked.

Alianora flushed. "N-n-nay," she stammered. "Ye must ha' misheard."

Carahue arched his brows, too polite to call her a liar in so many words. She moved her own horse beside his until knees touched. "This is a wearisome journey," she murmured. "Will ye no beguile our way with some further tale o' your exploits? Ye've done *so* many bold deeds, and ye relate them *so* well."

"Oh, now . . . Ahem!" Carahue grinned, twirled his mustache, and launched into a recital. The girl listened wide-eyed to the most outrageous, if smoothly phrased, brags that Holger had heard in his life. Presently her respectful oh's and ah's got too much for the Dane to bear. He jerked harshly on Papillon's reins and rode to one side by himself. The pleasure of his victory had quite departed.

21

EVENING FOUND THEM under the pass. It proved to be an upward gash through the cliff, covered deep with sharded rock, where the mountain had been faulted. The climb to the plateau next day would take hours. Thereafter, Alianora said, they would not lack many miles of their goal, and travel should be easy.

Easy as the descent to hell, Holger thought with a shiver. The agnostic engineer in him observed that so far the path had been more like the proverbial road to heaven. But the engineer's world seemed infinitely far away, in time as well as in space, a dream he had once had, fading out of his memory as all dreams must.

Beneath the precipices they found a meadow, if that patch of soil was not too barren to rate the name, and established camp. In the center loomed a tall monolith. It might have been a pagan menhir, before the troll that Hugi smelled came to nest in some nearby cave and drive humans away. Darkness clamped down. The wind had resumed, and strengthened hourly. Orange flames streamed along the ground; sparks flew off like meteors and were as swiftly snuffed. Overhead lay a blackness where the gibbous moon was seen in rare glimpses, racing among monstrous cloud shapes. The night was full of whistlings, rustlings, and croakings.

The party were too exhausted to do more than swallow a little food and roll up in their blankets. Hugi took the first watch, Holger the second. By that time the night was absolute. Holger poked the fire, drew his cloak tightly about him against the cold, and looked down at his companions.

The blaze picked them out in guttering highlights. Carahue slept like a cat, as quiet and easy as when he was awake. Hugi had rolled himself into a cocoon of blanket from which only his lustily snoring nose projected. Holger's eyes went to Alianora and remained there. The blanket had slid off her. She lay on her side, legs drawn up and hands clasped over the small breasts. Her face, glimpsed through a tangle of hair, was childlike, blind with sleep, a strangely helpless look. Holger stooped to tuck her in. His lips brushed her cheek and she smiled without waking.

He rose. A heaviness was in him, more for her than himself. If he had been snatched by irresistible warring powers, too bad, but he hated the thought of her being whirled along with him, he knew not whither. What could he do, though? What could he do?

He struck one fist into the other palm. "God damn it," he mumbled, "God damn it," and didn't know if he cursed or implored.

"Holger."

He jerked around. The sword leaped into his hand. Nothing met his glare but murk, out beyond the firelight. The wind blew, the dry grass murmured, somewhere an owl screamed.

"Holger."

He trod to the edge of the charmed circle. "Who's that?" Despite himself, he spoke softly.

"Holger," said the voice. "Do not call out. You are the only one I would speak with."

His pulses sprang. The sword dropped, as if grown too heavy for him. Morgan le Fay walked into the light.

It wavered, painting her red against blackness. Shadows caressed the body within the fluttering long dress. The fire touched her eyes and lit tiny flames therein. "What do you want?" Holger husked.

Her smile was slow and beautiful. "Only to speak with you. Come here to me."

"No." He shook his head violently, hoping to clear it. "Nothing doing. I won't step beyond the circle."

"You need have no fear. At least, not of any beings whom your symbols would halt. They are elsewhere, readying for battle." She shrugged. "But do as you wish."

"What have you got, then, to threaten me with?" he asked. "More cannibals?"

"Those whom you met today were under my command to take you alive at any cost," she said earnestly. "You would have done best to yield to them. They would have borne you to me, unharmed."

"And my friends?"

"What are those acquaintances of a few weeks to you, Holger? Why should you care? Remember, in any case, my dear one, that party whom you routed today have returned to the main army of their tribe. Their chief is crazed with rage at the shame you put upon him. Not I nor hell itself could stop him from seeking to kill, when next he meets you. His honor can only be regained by eating your heart. Come away with me, Holger, while you can."

"With you, who helped teach those poor savages to eat men?"

She grimaced. "That was not I. Certain allies of mine, the demons and their prophets whom Chaos has used to bring the hillmen under our control . . . they have preached an uncouth religion. Not one that I would have taught." Her smile returned. "My belief is in joy, in the fulfillment of life, that which I taught you once and would fain teach you again, Holger."

"That argument won't work either," he said. He looked past her, into night. This time, he suddenly realized, he meant it. He did not desire Morgan le Fay. When she reached out and took his hand, her fingers might have been any woman's. An attractive woman, certainly, but no more than that.

"You are not the most constant person in the world," she said, still smiling. "Once you revolted against your own liege lord, Carl himself. He never had a fiercer enemy, before your own large-heartedness ended the feud."

"But we were reconciled, I gather." He withdrew his hand from her clasp.

She glanced at Alianora. Her sigh held an unfeigned sadness. "I perceive an older witchcraft than mine has ensorcelled you, Holger. Welladay, 'twas joyous once. Nothing can take that from me."

"You took my past from *me*," he said bitterly. "You made me into a child again and sent me out of my whole universe. It's not your doing I've come back. Something else brought me, that neither of us understands."

"So you know that much," she said. "Would you know yet more? I can return to you those lost memories, if you wish."

"At what price? The same you wanted last time?"

"Less. You need not even betray your friends here. I could see to it that they also prosper. Your present course will only lead them to destruction with you."

"How can I trust your word?"

"Let me restore your memory. Come out of the circle that I may use a spell to dissolve the murk in you. Then you will recall what oaths are binding on me."

He moved his gaze back to her. Tall and serene she stood, except for the dark hair that tossed under her coronet. Yet he sensed how she

was drawn tense as a wire about to break. The full mouth had grown
thin, the curved nose dilated, the fire reflections in her eyes leaped
feverish. Slowly, her fists clenched.

And why should the world's greatest witch fear him?

He pondered it, standing there in the windy night with sleep at his
feet and blackness overhead. She had powers, yes, and she had used
them against him; but he himself was charged with some other, opposing
force, and there was that which said, "Thus far and no farther." All the
magics they had tried, in Avalon, in Faerie, in mortal lands, had failed
to halt him. Now even her own beauty had been made impotent by gray
eyes and brown tresses. She had no enchantments remaining that could
stop him.

Of course, to something which was not hexed up by her but was
supernatural in its own right—or to ordinary cold steel—he was still
terribly mortal.

"In my world," he said wonderingly, "you're a myth. I never
thought I'd fight a myth."

"That was not your world either," she said. "There, you too are a
legend. This is your place, here with me."

He shook his head. "Both worlds are mine, I think," he answered
stolidly. "Somehow I have a place in both."

Nevertheless, excitement rose in him. He'd been too preoccupied to
draw the obvious conclusion before this instant: that he himself belonged to the Carolingian-Arthurian cycle. Somewhere back in that other
cosmos (how far from this night and this woman!) he might once have
read of his own deeds.

But if so, he decided drearily, the forgetfulness had covered it. His
name might be a household word at home; he might have been his own
boyhood hero; but Morgan's spell continued to work. The transition here
had blanked out whatever recollections he had had of any stories about
. . . about three hearts and three lions.

"Meseems, at least you like this world best," said Morgan. "Beware
lest you blunder back into the other." She made a step closer to him,
until they almost touched. "Aye, there is indeed a great hosting in both
worlds, and you are the crux in both. I'll confess that much. But if you
go through with this crazy scheme, wielding powers you know nothing
of, you'll most likely fail and die. Or you will perchance succeed, and
rue that you did. Lay down your burden now, Holger, and abide here
happy forever. There is still time!"

He grinned with little humor. "You wouldn't try so hard to talk me
into quitting, if my chance of winning weren't better than you let on,"
he said. "I suppose you know where I'm bound. You've done your best

to fool me, and capture me, and cripple me. No doubt you'll try next to kill me. But I mean to keep going."

What highfalutin words, gibed his inward self. *A fellow would almost think you meant them.*

He knew in an uprush of weariness that he only wanted peace. An end to this warring in the dark. A place to hide with Alianora from all the worlds and all their cruelties. But he couldn't so much as ask for a rest. There were too many others who would get trampled underfoot, the moment he was out of the way. He was no damned hero, but Judas, a guy had to live with himself, didn't he?

Morgan watched him for a long moment. The wind whistled around them. "There is fate in this," she said at last, heavily. "Yes, I see that even Carahue has returned. The parts of the pattern are gathered. But do not be sure that the Weaver will complete it."

Sudden tears glimmered in her eyes. She leaned forward and kissed him, not hard, almost fleetingly, but he had seldom felt a greater tenderness. "Good-by, Holger," she said. She turned and walked out of sight.

He stood and shivered in the cold. Ought he to call the others? No, let them sleep, he thought vaguely. He didn't want to talk about what had happened. Nobody's damn business.

Time passed. The night hooted louder. He stirred from his reverie with a glance upward, to gauge from the moon if his watch was over. The sky was an inkpot of clouds. No matter. He might as well stay on guard. He wouldn't sleep anyhow, after what had happened. Not to mention the noise. A real gale was blowing now, stones rattled, metal clinked——

Hey!

The cannibal chief bounded into sight. Beyond him flashed spearheads. There must be a hundred or more men, they'd lain doggo in the pass and now Morgan had sent them down to— "Wake up! Wake up, here they come!"

Hugi, Carahue, and Alianora scrambled to their feet. The Saracen's blade snaked free. He sprang toward his startled horse and ripped the reins from the tethering stake. The girl jumped onto her mount. Two hillmen whooped and plunged at her. One thrust with a spear. Hugi dove between his legs, a tiny brown hurricane. They went down together. Holger pounced on the other. His sword rose and fell. A skull split hideously.

As the body pitched against him, he threw it back hard enough to bowl over the next man. A spear grated along his chain mail. He hacked out at the chief's face. Dim in the firelight, filed teeth grinned at him.

Arms closed around his neck. He kicked backward, making vicious use of his spurs. The savage yammered and let go.

Holger retreated till he had the menhir behind him. A tall man with a dragon painted on his stomach leaped to attack. Holger cut sideways. The man's head rolled from its shoulders. A ring of other men pressed close. Beyond their feathers and horns, he saw Carahue mounted, slashing downward with his saber. Papillon kicked, bit, stamped; mane and tail flew like black flames.

A hillman rose up, belly to belly with Holger. He had slithered under the Dane's guard. The dagger in his hand spurted upward. Holger managed to take the slash on his left arm. Then Hugi appeared below the savage, grabbed his ankles and threw him. Man and dwarf rolled over, snarling and gouging.

The chief had been immediately behind. His ax smote Holger's helmet with a thundercrack noise. Holger lurched. "God and St. George," he heard himself groan. The chief laughed and struck again. Somehow Holger parried the blows. Most of them. Others banged on his helmet and hauberk. He reeled. Two more men rushed in from the sides.

Carahue appeared behind them. The Saracen's blade whined. A heathen clutched his own arm, stared stupidly as it came off in his hand, and went to his knees. Holger cut low and got the leg of the other, who stumbled back. The chief whirled to engage Carahue with his ax. They clanged about, cursing.

Alianora's horse screamed. Hamstrung, it sank to earth. The white swan flew up, swooped down again to peck at eyes. Holger sobbed breath into his lungs. Someone yammered an order. Hurled spears flew thick around him. He forgot he was hurt and exhausted. He charged. His blade went like a scythe. Papillon reared inhumanly big, dashed out brains with his forefeet and overrode war cries with his neighing. Man and horse scattered the band of javelin throwers and returned to the stone.

Hugi rose from a body gone limp, dusted his hands, and joined them. Alianora turned woman again at the same place. A moment afterward Carahue cantered up. Holger put foot in stirrup and mounted Papillon. A savage rushed him. He kicked the fellow's teeth in. Bending, he got his shield on his arm. His sword hand he extended long enough to help Alianora up behind him. Carahue gave a seat to Hugi. The two knights looked at each other, nodded, and rode to battle.

For a few minutes it was slash and stab and hew. Then all at once the enemy was gone. Holger and Carahue returned to the menhir and gasped. Their swords ran red. Blood was spattered across clothes and arms and faces. The firelight gleamed off blood puddles on the earth. Bodies lay strewn, some moving and moaning, some altogether still. The hillmen were drawn into a sullen clump on the edge of vision; only their weapons could really be seen. Holger recognized the chief, whose war bonnet was gone and whose scalp was lacerated. The chief picked himself off the ground and hobbled toward his men.

Carahue's grin flashed out. "Nobly, nobly done!" he panted. "By the hand of the Prophet . . . the Prophet Jesus, Sir Rupert, I thought only one man in the world could fight as you have done!"

"You're no slouch yourself," said Holger. "But I wish you'd been able to finish their boss. He'll work them up to another attack in a minute."

"Arrows'll end us," declared Hugi. "Had they any sense, they loons would ha' made pincushions o' us erenow."

Holger looked back at Alianora. Blood ran from her left arm. The fear that leaped into him was horrible. "Are you hurt?" he cried, shrill as a woman.

"Nay, 'tis naught." She smiled with shaking lips. "A dart did but wing me."

He fumbled at the wound. A bad gash ordinarily, he'd have said; but not much considering the present circumstances. His bones seemed to melt. "I'll build a chapel . . . to St. Sebastian . . . for this," he whispered.

Her hands closed about his waist. "There's a better way ye micht show gladness," she said, low and close to his ear.

Carahue interrupted brusquely, "We'll be in no state to build anything unless we escape soon. If we rush downhill, Rupert, we may elude pursuit."

The moltenness in Holger congealed. "No," he said. "That's no good. This is the way to St. Grimmin's. The other passes are beset, even if we had time to seek them out. We have to cross here."

"Straight through them?" spat the Saracen. "Trying to climb that scree in the dark, with a hundred warriors attacking? Now your wits have boiled away."

"You can flee if you wish," said Holger, out of the ice within him. "I have to reach the church this night."

Hugi stared at him, until he squirmed beneath those beady eyes and snapped, "Well, what ails you? We'll probably die in the pass. I know it. Run off with Carahue. I'll go alone."

"Nay," said Hugi.

They fell so still that Holger heard the blood beat in his own veins. The dwarf spoke low and harsh: "Sith ye be boon to mak' a knightly fool o' yersel', I can at least ease yer gowkishness for ye. Well ye know we canna get through yon pass. Yet there's another way onto the wold, where they uns will ne'er follow. I can snuff our way to the troll's burrow. 'Tis na far off, says ma nase. Sure 'tis he'll ha' more nor ane passage leading above the cliffs; and mayhap he'll be abroad, or asleep, or far off in his tunnels, and willna grow 'ware of us. 'Tis a horrid chance to take, but methinks oor ainly chance. What say ye? Is 't that big a rush to reach the haunted kirk?"

Holger heard a gasp at his back. "Carahue," he said, "take Alianora and see if you can get her to safety. Hugi and I'll have a go at that troll hole——"

The girl seized his belt. "Nay," she said angrily, "ye'll no be rid o' me so easy. I come too."

"And I," said Carahue after a gulp or three. "Never yet have I shirked an adventure."

"Horse apples!" snorted Hugi. "Yer bones will be scattered in the troll's nest. Ye're no the first twa knichts wha' died because they had so bluidy much pride there was na room left for brains. I'm nobbut grieved that ye maun drag the swan-may doon wi' ye. Noo, mak' ready to gallop!"

22

CARAHUE LED THE WAY, with Hugi for guide. The mare took off in a clatter. For a moment Holger was aware of the red and blue ribbons twined into her flowing tail. Then Papillon's muscles surged between his knees.

Headed east along the scarp, they must pass the enemy. A howl arose. Holger saw a spear fly from the left. As its head caught what firelight there was, he saw it turn in the air and arch downward. He raised his shield. The spear rebounded. An instant later, three arrows thunked solidly into the wooden frame.

He rushed on into the gloom beyond. The white mare and the loose white clothes of her rider were a blob, scarcely to be told from shadows. Papillon stumbled. Sparks showered where horseshoes chipped flint. Perforce, the animals slowed to an even trot. On both sides and overhead Holger was blind. He didn't know if his imagination or his senses told him of the cliffs to the left. He felt their weight loom above him, crushingly, as if he were already buried beneath.

A glance behind etched the heathen leader on his vision. The gaunt man in the badger mantle had snatched a brand from the campfire. He whirled it over his head till flames blossomed and he stood forth startlingly red and yellow. With a cry to his warriors he raised his ax and bounded in chase.

Swiftly he overtook the horses. Holger glimpsed others following, not quite so eager. But his attention was on this man. The chief approached on the left side, where the knight's sword couldn't reach. He darted in and chopped at Papillon's fetlock. The stallion skittered away, nearly throwing his riders. Holger whirled him about to face the next attack.

If I'm delayed here longer than a minute, the bunch of 'em will surround me, the Dane realized. "Hang on, Alianora!" He leaned far over and slashed at his opponent. His blow was parried by the ax. Nimbler than any charger, the cannibal moved back. The painted face with the braided beard mocked at Holger.

But the torch in his left hand remained in sword range. Holger swatted it against the hillman's breast. The savage barked with pain. Before he could recover, Holger was close enough to chop once more. This time the steel met flesh. The chief went down.

You poor, brave bastard, Holger thought. He spurred Papillon after Carahue. The encounter had only taken seconds.

They moved on through endlessness. The enemy trailed them, not venturing to rush. Arrows zipped through the dark. Whoops ululated. "They'll rally themselves soon enough and close in on us," Carahue said over his shoulder.

"I think no," said Alianora. "Canna ye whiff?"

Holger strained his nostrils. The wind was more or less in his face. He heard it go *whoo-oo* and shake his plume and cloak; he felt how chill it was. Nothing more.

"Ugh!" said Carahue a minute later. "Is that what I smell?"

Someone wailed in the night behind. Holger's tobacco-dulled nose was the last to catch the odor. By that time the cannibals had given up the pursuit. They'd doubtless stick around to make sure next morning that their foes had not doubled back downhill; but they were going no farther in this direction.

If a smell could be called thick and cold, one might describe the troll's. When Holger reached the cave mouth, he gagged.

He drew rein. Alianora leaped to the ground. "We must gather stuff for faggots, to licht our way," she explained. "I feel dry twigs lying about, belike dropped from armfuls the beast carried hither to make his nest." Presently she had a bundle to which Hugi sent flint and steel. As the flames grew, Holger saw a ten-foot hole in the cliff wall. Lightlessness gaped beyond.

He and Carahue had dismounted. They gave Alianora their horses to lead at the rear. They themselves went in the forefront, with Hugi for torchbearer. "Well," said the Dane uselessly, "here we go." His tongue was dry.

"I would we micht see the stars once more," Alianora said. The wind blew her words away. Hugi squeezed her hand.

"Oh, come now," said Carahue. "Suppose we do meet the troll? Our swords will cut him to flitches. Methinks we're funking at an old wives' tale." He strode briskly to the cave entrance, and through.

Holger went along. The sword in his right fist, the shield on his left arm, were heavy. He felt sweat trickling under his mail, itches he couldn't scratch, dull aches where blows had landed. The air in the cave was full of troll and carrion smells. The faggot flames danced, sank low, flickered high again, so that shadows bobbed across the rough walls. Holger could have sworn some of the formations were faces that mouthed at him. Underfoot were stones on which he stubbed his toes. Alianora foresightedly continued to pick up bits of wood and straw, among the animal bones scattered along the way. The loudest noise was of horseshoes, a sharp clopping followed by hollow echoes. More and more, Holger had a sense of walls that pressed inward.

At the end of the cave a tunnel had been dug, nine feet high and not much wider, so that Holger and Carahue were crowded close. Holger tried not to wonder if the troll had dug it out barehanded. Once or twice he kicked recognizable pieces of human skulls. After the tunnel had dipped a few times his sense of balance quit and he *knew* they were headed downward, endlessly downward, into the guts of the earth. He strangled a wish to scream.

The passage debouched in a slightly larger cavern. Three other holes opened on the far side. Hugi waved his companions back and stumped around. The torchlight threw his face into craggy prominences but painted his shadow behind, like a black grotesque thing about to eat him.

He studied the flame, which had turned yellow and smoky; he wet his thumb and held it this way and that; he stooped to smell the ground. Finally he looked at the left-hand exit. "This ane," he grunted.

"No," Holger said. "Can't you see the floor slants down in that direction?"

"Nay, it doesna. Mak' no such muckle noise."

"You're nuts, I tell you!" Holger protested. "Any fool——"

Hugi stared through his brows at the man. "Any fool can follow his ain fancy," the dwarf said. "Mayhap ye're richt. I canna say for certain. But 'tis ma opinion that yon tunnel's wha' we want, and I ken a bit more to burrowing than ye do. So, are ye man eneugh to heed?"

Holger swallowed. "Okay," he said. "I'm sorry. Lead on."

A ghost of a smile lifted Hugi's whiskers. "Guid lad." He trotted into the passage he had chosen. The rest followed.

Before long the way bent unmistakably upward. Holger said nothing when Hugi passed several holes without a glance. But when he came to another triple choice, the dwarf cast about for minutes.

In the end, troubled, he said, "By every token, we maun tak, the middle o' those. Yet meseems the troll stink is strongest thither."

"You can tell a difference?" said Carahue wryly.

"Mayhap his nest lies in yon direction," Alianora whispered. A horse blew out its lips: in that narrow, resonant space, a gunshot noise. "Could ye no find us a roundabout way?"

"Mayhap," said Hugi doubtfully. " 'Twould tak' a lang whiles."

"And we've got to reach the church soon," Holger said.

"Why?" asked Carahue.

"Never mind now," said Holger. "Will you believe me on my word?"

This was no place to stop and explain the complicated truth, however trustworthy the Saracen had proven himself. But the obvious fact was, the sword Cortana was crucial. The enemy wouldn't have striven so hard to block this quest, were it a wild goose chase.

Morgan could get to the church ahead of him without trouble. However, then she couldn't shift the weapon elsewhere. Doubtless it was too heavy for her natural strength and too holy for her spells. She would need human assistance, as she had had when Cortana was first stolen. But by all accounts, the heathen were too frightened of St. Grimmin's church to go near, even at her command; and her men elsewhere in the world were too busy preparing to march on the Empire.

Still, given time she could certainly find someone. Or . . . more likely . . . she could summon Powers that would intercept Holger on his route. He'd been luckier so far than he deserved; he knew damn well he couldn't fight his way through her ultimate allies. Only a saint could do that, and he was a long way from sainthood.

Q.E.D.: he had to make haste.

Carahue's gaze rested gravely on him before the Moor said, "As you wish, my friend. Let us take the straightest path, then."

Hugi shrugged and led on. The burrow twisted, rose, dipped, rose again, cornered, writhed, widened and narrowed. Their footfalls sounded like drumbeats. *Here, here, here we are, troll. Here, here, here we are.*

When the rock walls closed in so they almost brushed each shoulder Holger found himself behind Hugi, with Carahue at his back and Alianora guiding the horses in line to the Saracen's rear. Before his eyes were only red-shot glooms as the torch sputtered. He heard Carahue murmur:

"The heaviest of my sins is that ever I let so sweet a maiden enter so foul a place. God will not forgive me this."

"But I will," she breathed.

He chuckled. "Heh! That suffices! And after all, my lady, who needs sun or moon or stars when you are present?"

"Nay, I beg ye, we must no talk."

"So I shall think instead. Thoughts of beauty, grace, gentleness, and charm: in a word, thoughts of Alianora."

"Och, Carahue——"

Holger bit his lip till the pain stabbed him.

"Quiet back there," Hugi rapped. "We've come to his very nest."

The tunnel ended. Torchlight would not reach far into the cavern beyond. Holger had confused glimpses of walls curving upward to lose themselves in a moving darkness. The floor was piled deep with branches, leaves, moldering straw, and bones: everywhere the gnawed bones. A stink of death overwhelmed him. He retched.

"Still, I say!" Hugi ordered. "Think ye I like this place? Noo, soft across yon space. There'll be exits aplenty on t' other side."

The carpeting crackled underfoot, louder for each step. Holger swayed in its thick unevenness. He tripped over a log. A branch scratched his cheek, as if trying for his eyes. A human chine fell apart when he trod on it. He heard the horses sink under their weight, wallow about and whicker indignantly.

The torch brightened. At the same moment Holger felt a cold draft. "Ho, we're na so far from the top!" Hugi exclaimed.

"Ho," went the echo. "Ho-o-o."

The troll crawled from beneath dead leaves.

Alianora screamed. Even then Holger thought he had never before heard real fear in her voice. "God have mercy," Carahue choked. Hugi crouched and snarled. Holger dropped his sword, stooped to get it, dropped it again as sweat spurted out of him.

The troll shambled closer. He was perhaps eight feet tall, perhaps more. His forward stoop, with arms dangling past thick claw-footed legs to the ground, made it hard to tell. The hairless green skin moved upon his body. His head was a gash of a mouth, a yard-long nose, and two eyes which were black pools, without pupil or white, eyes which drank the feeble torchlight and never gave back a gleam.

"Ho-o-o," he grinned, and reached out his hand.

Carahue shouted. The saber flared. It struck with a butcher sound. Smoke rose from the wound. The troll's smirk did not change. He reached the other hand toward Carahue. Holger got his sword and attacked that arm.

The troll batted at him. Holger caught the blow on his shield. The wood cracked. He tumbled into the rotten heap on the floor. A moment he lay struggling for breath. Carahue's mare shrieked in panic and plunged about. Alianora hung from the reins. That much Holger saw before he got back to his feet. Then his gaze focused on Carahue.

The Saracen danced over the nest. Incredibly, he kept his balance in that tangle. Each clumsy lunge he dodged, ducked, and never did his sword rest. It whistled and clamored, a blur, behind which he smiled. Each blow went far into green flesh. The troll only grunted. But Carahue continued to seek the right wrist, coldly and carefully.

Until with a final blow he lopped off that hand.

"Next!" he laughed aloud. "Give us some light, Hugi!" The dwarf had stuck the faggot upright between two branches and now tried to help Alianora control the mare. Papillon circled about looking for a chance to help.

The stallion got his chance as the troll made a left-handed swipe at Carahue. He rushed from behind. His front hoofs smote the broad back with a drumbeat fury. The troll went on his face, Papillon reared to his full terrifying height and came down again. The troll's head was shattered.

"Merciful heaven," gasped Carahue. He crossed himself. Turning to Holger, he called gaily, "That wasn't too bad, though, was it?"

Holger looked at his own caved-in shield. "No," he said in a rueful mood. "Except for my own performance."

The mare still shivered, but had calmed enough for Alianora to stroke her neck. "Come, let's gang on oot," said Hugi. "The fetor here's like to melt ma nase."

Holger nodded. "Shouldn't be far—*Jesu Kriste!*"

Like a huge green spider, the troll's severed hand ran on its fingers. Across the mounded floor, up onto a log with one taloned forefinger to hook it over the bark, down again it scrambled, until it found the cut wrist. And there it grew fast. The troll's smashed head seethed and knit together. He clambered back on his feet and grinned at them. The waning faggot cast red light over his fangs.

He lumbered toward Holger. The Dane knew a moment's blind wish to bolt. But there was no place to go. He spat on the ground and lifted his sword. As the troll reached for him, he swung with all the might he had.

Through and through that oak-branch arm the blade went. Iron belled in the dark. Ice-green blood spurted, turning black in the smoke of unnatural flesh. The sword seemed to glow. The arm sprang off at the shoulder. It rolled into a pile of leaves, flopped about, and began hunching its way back.

Carahue smote from the right side. His saber carved a slab off the troll's ribs. Greasily, with a sucking noise, that chunk crawled toward its master. Papillon reared and smote with his forefeet. Half the troll's face was torn off. The jaws landed under the stallion and clenched about his ankle. He neighed and bucked. The troll raked his haunches with the remaining hand. Blood welled forth. Carahue got in the way of another buffet, took it in the armored belly, went down with a clatter and did not rise.

Unkillable indeed! Holger thought. *What a place to die.* "Get out, Alianora!"

"Nay." She grabbed the torch and neared Papillon, who was going mad with the grip on his leg. "I'll get it from ye," she shouted. "Hold still and I'll free ye."

The troll scooped up his left arm and put it in place. His half a face seemed still to laugh. Holger struck again and again, he opened deep wounds, but they closed at once. Back he stumbled. Over the troll's shoulder he saw Alianora duck under Papillon's flailing hoofs, seize the stallion's bridle and somehow bring him to a halt. She knelt to try and pry the jaws loose.

As her torch came near, they let go. Startled, she flinched aside. "Ho-o-o," said the troll. Turning from Holger, he scuttled toward the bones, picked them up and put them in his head. Teeth clashed as he went back to meet the Dane.

Alianora cried aloud. She struck his back with the torch. He hooted and went on all fours. A charred welt across his skin did not heal.

The knowledge burst open in Holger. "Fire!" he roared. "Light a fire! Burn the beast!"

Alianora plunged the faggot into a heap of straw. It flared up. Smoke stung Holger's nose . . . clean smoke, he thought crazily, clean flames, burning out the tomb stench around him. He braced himself and hewed.

A hand flew off its wrist, halfway across the cavern. Alianora pounced on it. The thing writhed in her grasp. Fingers like green worms sought to claw free. She hurled it into the fire. For a moment the hand twisted about, even crawled from the flames. But it was already blackened. As it sank down dead, the fire moved out to engulf it.

The troll yammered. He swung the mutilated arm like a club. The sword was knocked from Holger's grasp. He scrambled after it. The troll overfell him. A moment he lay under that mass and could not breathe. Papillon attacked. The monster retreated.

Carahue staggered erect and went to battle. Papillon had the troll down. Carahue chopped at a leg, again and yet again. When he got it off, Alianora seized it in both arms. The fire was catching in wood now. Its crackle had become a bellow; it filled the cave with light. She needed her entire strength, but she pushed the kicking leg in among the coals.

Holger came back. A hand closed on his ankle . . . the other hand cut off by Carahue. He tore it loose and threw it at the fire. Somehow it landed in the clear and pulled itself toward safety under a log. Hugi dove upon it. They rolled over together, dwarf and hand.

The troll's head was off. It snapped and slobbered as Holger spitted it on his sword. He tossed it into the blaze. It rolled back, burning, spreading the flames, toward Alianora. Holger stabbed it again. Heedless of what would happen to the temper of his blade, he pinned the troll's head in the fire till it was consumed.

The torso remained. Worst was that task, when Holger and Carahue rolled a thing as heavy as the world toward the furnace heart of the cave, while it fought them with snakes of gut. Afterward he could not remember clearly what had happened. But they burned it.

A last glimmer caught his eye. Red and ragged as the flames themselves, Hugi cast the troll's hand into destruction. Then he sank to the floor and lay still.

Alianora flung herself above him. "He's bad hurt," she cried. Holger could scarcely hear her through the conflagration. Heat and fumes made him too dizzy to think. "Hugi, Hugi!"

"We'd best escape before this whole place becomes a cauldron," Carahue panted in Holger's ear. "See how the smoke rushes out yonder tunnel. That must be our way. Let her carry the dwarf. Help me with this idiot horse of mine!"

Somehow they quieted the animal. Somehow they groped their way down a passage where each breath was pain. And they came into the open air.

23

THEY WERE ABOVE the cliffs, Holger realized with a dull surprise. How long they had been underground he didn't know, but the moon was westering.

The moon? Oh, yes. Yes, the clouds were breaking up, weren't they? Too much wind for them. The wind went shrieking across a plain of whins and stiff grass, here and there a leafless tree, everything gray under hurried moonlight and unmercifully sharp stars. Holger couldn't see the smoke from the troll's bolthole; the wind scattered it too fast. Southward, close at hand, the wold was bounded by the cliff brink, beyond which he saw nothing save darkness, as if he stood at the edge of creation. Northward he thought mountains shouldered the sky, a blink of glaciers, but he wasn't sure. The chill struck into his marrow.

Carahue limped to join him. Holger wondered if he looked as bad as the Saracen, torn, smeared with blood, black with smoke, in dented helmet and ripped clothes, carrying a ruined sword. Just as well the light was dim. A cloud engulfed the moon and he could not see at all.

"Is everyone here?" he croaked.

Carahue answered so low that the rushing in the grass nearly buried his voice. "I fear the little man came off badly."

"Nay," said the remnant of a bass growl. "I gave's guid as I got."

The moon broke free again. Holger knelt down beside Alianora. She cradled Hugi's shaggy head in her lap. Blood pulsed from the dwarf's side, but the flow ebbed even as Holger watched.

"Hugi," she whispered. "Ye canna die. I'll no believe it."

"Nay, lass, dinna fash yersel'," he mumbled. "Yon great galoon paid top price for me."

Holger bent close. In the white unreal moonlight the face below him was like a carving in old dark wood. Only the beard, windblown, and a few bubbles of blood on the lips, still moved. He saw the wound could not be staunched. It was too big for so small a body.

Hugi reached around and patted Alianora's hand. "Och, dinna weep," he sighed. " 'Tis about fifty females o' ma ain race wha' ha' cause to mourn. Yet 'twas ever ye who we loved best." He snapped after air. "I'd gi' ye guid counsel if I could. But the noise in ma head's too great."

Holger took off his helmet. *"Ave Maria,"* he began. There was nothing else he could do, and perhaps nothing better, here on this windy cold mountain. He asked that there be gentleness for the soul of Hugi. And when the dwarf was dead, Holger closed his eyes and signed him with the cross.

Rising, he left Alianora alone for the while that he and Carahue took to dig a shallow grave with their swords. Afterward they heaped rocks above, and stabbed Hugi's dagger into the cairn with the hilt up. Wolves howled, miles away on the wold. Holger hoped they wouldn't find the grave.

Finally the humans bound their own wounds as best they could. "We've had heavy losses," said Carahue. His gaiety was flattened out by weariness. "Not alone our friend, but a horse and the pack mule with its gear. Our swords are no more than edgeless iron clubs, our mail nearly beaten to pieces. Nor can Alianora fly until her wing . . . her arm heals."

Holger looked across the tumbled gray land. The wind struck him in the face. "This was my job," he said. "I don't feel right about anyone else getting hurt."

The Saracen regarded him steadily. "Methinks 'tis the task of all honorable men," he said.

"Look, Carahue, I may as well tell you we're being opposed by Queen Morgan le Fay herself. She'll know we came this far. I think she's already off to the Middle World to get those who can stop us."

"They travel fast, the Middle Worlders," said Carahue. "We'd best not stay to rest. But when we get to the church, what then?"

"Then my search is ended . . . perhaps . . . and maybe we'll be safe. Or maybe not. I don't know."

It was on Holger's tongue to tell Carahue the whole story, but the Saracen had already swung about and caught his horse. No time, no time.

Alianora sprang up behind Holger on Papillon. Her arms closed about his waist with a desperate tightness. Once only she turned, to wave at him who lay buried.

Even the stallion was worn out, and the mare shambled in her exhaustion. Hoofs rang on stone, grass parted with dry whisperings, the gorse rattled and the dead trees creaked. Low above the horizon, the crooked moon dazzled Holger's eyes, as if trying to blind him.

After a long while Alianora said, "Did the foe come on us by accident, below the pass?"

"No." Holger threw a glance across the colorless, shadow-stippled earth. Carahue was a silhouette against stars and clouds—probably sleeping in the saddle, for he made no response as Holger went on, "Morgan came first. She sent the tribesmen after we'd spoken."

"Wha' did she say to ye, yon witch?"

"She . . . nothing. She just wanted me to surrender."

"I think she hankered after more," said the girl. "She was your leman once, no?"

"Yes," said Holger dully.

"She could gi' ye a proud life."

"I told her I'd rather stay with you."

"Oh, my darling!" she whispered. "I—I——"

He heard her trying not to weep. "What's the matter?" he asked.

"Och, I dinna know. I shouldna be so happy now, should I, so soon? And, and, and yet I canna help it——" She wiped her eyes on the remnant of his cloak.

"But," he stuttered. "But. I mean you and Carahue."

"Him? A pleasant one, aye. Did ye really think, though, Holger, could ye really believe I wanted to do more than keep his mind off ye and your secret? And maybe make ye a wee bit jealous? How could any lass want any man save ye?"

He gaped at the Pole Star.

She caught her breath and laid her hands on his shoulders. "Now we'll gabble no more o' that," she said firmly. "But if ever I catch ye pawing at some wench again, Holger, 'twill go ill with ye." She paused. "Some wench beside me, 'tis."

He jerked his horse to a stop. "Carahue!" he called. "Wake up!"

"Ah?" The Saracen reached for his saber.

"Our animals," Holger said, not altogether speciously. "If we don't give them a rest, they'll keel over. We'll make better speed in the long run if we take an hour's break now."

The other man's face was an oval blur, his armor a dull sheen, but he could be seen to ponder. "I know not. Once Morgan rouses the pursuit against us, such horses go like a gale. And yet——" He shrugged. "As you wish."

They slid to the grass. Alianora tugged eagerly at Holger's hand.

He nodded to Carahue, hoping his gesture wasn't too smug. The Saracen looked startled for a moment, until he laughed. "Good fortune to you, my friend," he said. He stretched himself full length on the ground and whistled a tune at the sky.

Holger followed Alianora a ways off. He had forgotten his own weariness and pain. The heart beat in him, not violently, a strong glad tone through his whole body. When they stopped, they clasped hands and stood looking at each other.

Moonlight flowed over the wold, gray, shadow-barred, glinting on rime. Such clouds as remained were luminous-edged; the stars shone between them. The wind was still loud, but Holger paid no heed. He saw Alianora as a shape of quicksilver, of sliding shadow and cool white light. Dewdrops sparkled in her hair and there was moonlight in her eyes.

"We may no ha' a chance to talk again," she said quietly.

"Maybe not," he answered.

"So let me say now I love ye."

"And I love you."

"Oh, my dearest——" She came to him and he held her close.

"I've been a fool," he said presently, wishing he could find better words. "I didn't know what I wanted. I thought when this was over I could go off and leave you. I was wrong."

She forgave him with her hands and lips and eyes.

"If we do come through, somehow," he said, "we'll never be apart again. This is where I belong. Here, with you."

Her tears caught the moonlight but her laugh was low and happy.

" 'Tis enough," she said.

He kissed her again.

Carahue's shout pulled them away. The noise flew torn in the wind, ringing and dying away across that lake of moonlight. "Quickly, come quickly, the huntsmen!"

24

FAR AND FAINT, at the very edge of hearing, the horns blew. They had the noise of wind and sea and great beating wings, a hawk voice, a raven voice. And Holger knew that the Wild Hunt was out and after him.

He vaulted up on Papillon. As the stallion burst into movement, he raised Alianora to her place behind. Carahue was already off. The white mare and the tattered white clothes of her rider flew ghostly in the low moonlight. Hoofs rang and thundered. They bent down to the long fleeing.

The moon was an argent glare in Holger's left eye. The wold slid past, darkness underfoot, flung stones and hissing brush, a rattle of branches like laughter. He felt the horse's muscles throb and swing between his thighs; he felt the girl's hands on his waist, guiding him in the direction she had spied out. His iron clashed on him, leather creaked, the wind shouted. Loudest came the labor of the horse's breathing.

Everywhere around were stars, but unthinkably remote in a black heaven. The Swan flashed overhead, the Milky Way spilled suns off its dim arch, Carl's Wain wheeled under the Pole; all the stars were cold. Northward he began to see the peaks of this range, sword sharp, sheathed in ice that gleamed under the moon. Behind him waxed lightlessness.

Gallop and gallop and gallop! Now Holger heard the wild horns closer, shrilling and wailing. Never had he heard such anguish as was blown on the horns of the damned. Through the cloven air he heard hoofs in the sky and the baying of immortal hounds. He leaned forward. His body swayed with Papillon's haste, his rein hand loose on the arched neck, his other hand gripped about Alianora's.

Swiftly, swiftly, over the rime-gray wold, under the last storm-clouds and the sinking moon, gallop, gallop, gallop. The sorrow of the huntsmen shrieked in his head. He shook himself and strained to see his goal. There was only the plain and the glacial mountains beyond.

Carahue began to lag. His mare tripped. He jerked her head up and roweled her. Holger thought he could hear the feet of the nightmare dogs. A lunatic yelling broke about him.

He looked behind, but Alianora's tossing hair hid those who followed. He thought he saw metal ablaze. And was that the clatter of dead men's bones?

"Hasten, hasten, best of horses! Oh, run, my comrade, run as no horses ever did erenow, for surely all men are pursued with us. Haste thee, my darling, for we ride against striding Time, we ride against marching Chaos. Ah, God be with thee, God strengthen thee to run!"

The horn blasts filled his skull. The hoofs and hounds and empty bones were at his back. Holger felt Papillon stumble. Alianora was almost thrown. He clung to her wrist and dragged her against him. Once more they rode.

Up ahead there, what was that, stark athwart the sky? The church of St. Grimmin—but the Wild Hunt howled and swept downward. He heard the clamor of huge winds, and saw murk before his eyes. *Jesu Kriste, I am not worthy, but help thou me.*

A wall stood in his way. Papillon gathered himself and sprang. As the huntsmen closed in on him, Holger felt such a cold as he had not dreamed could be, strike through his heart. He thought he heard the wind whistle between his ribs.

The black stallion hit earth with a crash that nearly slammed him from the saddle. Carahue followed. The white mare did not clear the wall. She fell back, but her rider leaped free. He caught the top of the wall and pulled himself over to land in the churchyard. Holger heard the mare cry out once, briefly and horribly, as the roaring overwhelmed her.

And then it was gone. The wind was gone too. Silence shot up like a scream.

Holger bent over. His hand shook, but he caught Carahue's as he already held Alianora's. They looked about them.

The yard was overgrown with grass and whins, through which crumbling headstones could be seen to ring the ruinous outline of the church. Fog drifted in tendrils, glowing white where the hunchback moon touched, with a dank smell of corruption. Holger felt how Alianora shivered in the chill.

He heard the sound as it came from the shadows behind the church.

It was the sound of a horse moving among the graves, a horse old and lame and weary unto death, stumbling among the graves as it sought him, and he whimpered in his throat. For he knew that this was the Hell Horse, and whoso looks upon it shall die.

Papillon could not make haste, here where the headstones reached out of weeds like fingers to pull him down. Carahue took the reins and led the stallion. They walked between the slabs, which leaned about in a drunkenness of neglect, the names long worn from their faces. The sound of the old lame horse grew louder, slipping and staggering through shadow to meet them.

Mists glimmered about the church of St. Grimmin's, thicker and thicker, as if they would hide it. Holger could just see that the steeple was fallen, the roof gone, the windows blindly agape. Slowly, feeling his way through the vapors and the tombstones, Carahue neared it.

The hoofs of the Hell Horse scrunched in ancient gravel. But this was the door of the church. Holger sprang down. Alianora huddled on Papillon's back. He lifted his arms and she fell into them. He carried her up the time-gnawed steps.

"You too," said Carahue gently, and led the stallion inside.

They halted in what had been the nave and looked toward the altar. The last moonlight poured over it. The crucifix was still there, high above the fallen chancel, and Holger could see Christ's face against the stars. He fell to his knees and took off his helmet. After a moment Carahue and Alianora joined him.

They heard the Hell Horse depart. As its clopping, limping hoof-beats dragged into silence, the faintest of breezes awoke and scattered the fog. Holger thought that the church was not dead, not defiled. It stood roofed with sky and walled with the living world; it stood as the sign of peace.

He rose and held Alianora to him. This, he knew, was the end of his search, and the knowledge was pain. His eyes dwelt on her upturned face before he kissed her.

Carahue spoke soft: "What have you in truth come here to find?"

Holger did not answer at once. He approached the altar. In the floor before the communion rail was a stone slab. When he touched the iron ring thereof, a remembered thrill went through him.

"This," he said. He drew his sword, which was now useless as a weapon, and slipped it through the ring for a lever. The slab was monstrously heavy. He felt the steel bend as he strained. "Help me," he gasped. "Oh, help me!"

Carahue thrust his own blade into the crack the Dane had opened. A moment afterward, the other sword broke across. Together they lifted the slab. It fell to the paving with a hollow thud and shattered in three pieces.

Alianora seized Holger's shoulder. "Listen!" she exclaimed.

He raised his head. Far off he heard the noise of an army. There was an earthquake hammering of hoofs, the sound of trumpets, the death-like clangor of arms. "It is the host of Chaos," he said, "riding forth on mankind."

He looked down into the narrow hole at his feet. Moonlight shone bluely off the great blade which lay waiting.

"We need not fear," he said. "In this sword is locked that before which they cannot stand. When their demon gods have been driven back into the Middle World, the human savages will despair and flee. We got here soon enough."

"Who are ye?" whispered Alianora.

"I don't know yet," he said. "But I shall."

A moment more he delayed. There was a Power in him, but it was something beyond man and man's hopes. He dared not lift the glaive.

He looked up at the figure on the cross. Bending, he took the sword Cortana in his hand.

"I know that blade," breathed Carahue.

Holger felt the illusion that masked him dissolve. And his memory returned and he knew himself.

They gathered around him, Alianora in the circle of his free arm, Carahue clasping his shoulder, Papillon's nose gentle against his cheek. "Whatever comes," he said, "whatever happens to me, know that you will return safe, and that you will always bear my love."

"I sought you, comrade," said Carahue. "I sought you, Ogier."

"I love ye, Holger," said Alianora.

Holger Danske, whom the old French chronicles know as *Ogier le Danois*, mounted into the saddle. And this was the prince of Denmark who in his cradle was given strength and luck and love by such of Faerie as wish men well. He it was who came to serve Carl the Great and rose to be among the finest of his knights, the defender of Christendie and mankind. He it was who smote Carahue of Mauretania in battle, and became his friend, and wandered far with him. He it was whom Morgan le Fay held dear; and when he grew old, she bore him to Avalon and gave him back his youth. There he dwelt until the paynim again menaced France, a hundred years later, and thence he sallied forth to conquer them anew. Then in the hour of his triumph he was carried away from mortal men.

And some say he waits in timeless Avalon until France the fair is in danger, and some say he sleeps beneath Kronborg Castle and wakens in the hour of Denmark's need, but none remember that he is and has always been a man, with the humble needs and loves of a man; to all, he is merely the Defender.

He rode out on the wold, and it was as if dawn rode with him.

NOTE

I HAD A LETTER from Holger Carlsen right after the war, to say he'd come through alive. After that I didn't hear from him until one day two years later, when he sauntered into my office.

I thought he'd changed a lot, grown more quiet and much older-looking, but wasn't too surprised considering what he must have experienced as an undergrounder. He explained that he'd gotten an American job again. "Just a money earner," he said. "What I really want to do is haunt your bookstores. I've located stuff in London and Paris and Rome, but not enough yet."

"What on earth?" I said. "You, a bibliophile?"

He laughed rather harshly. "Not quite. I'll tell you some other time." He went on to ask about mutual friends from the old days. His London stay had improved his English.

The other time wasn't long about coming, though. I imagine he wanted a sympathetic audience quite badly. He'd been received into the Catholic Church—a datum which, knowing him, I advance as important evidence in favor of this story—but of course the confessional booth doesn't serve the same purpose. He needed to tell the whole thing, as it had been for him. "Not that I expect you to believe a word of this," he said, over beer and sandwiches one midnight in my apartment. "Only listen, will you?"

He finished in the darkness before morning, when the streets lay empty beneath us and the city's lights were so muted we could see a few stars. He poured himself more beer and stared at it for a long while before he drank.

"And how did you get back?" I asked, most quietly, so as not to jar him. He looked like a sleepwalker.

"Suddenly I *was* back," he said. "I rode out and scattered the hosts of Chaos, driving them before me. And somehow it began to seem as if I were also fighting on that beach, in another night and another world. And then I was. I rushed forward, naked. My clothes hadn't made the transition with me, you see, and lay in a heap at my feet. A bullet or two grazed me, but nothing worse. I was moving so damn fast. Faster than human flesh has a right to move. The doctors say that can happen under conditions of extreme stress. Adrenalin or something. Anyhow, I got in among the Germans, took his gun away from one of them, clubbed it, and went to work. The business was soon over."

He grimaced at an unpleasant recollection, but said doggedly, "Those two worlds—and many more, for all I know—are in some way the same. The same fight was being waged, here the Nazis and there the Middle World; but in both places, Chaos against Law, something old and wild and blind at war with man and the works of man. In both worlds it was the time of need for Denmark and France. So Ogier came forth in both of them, as he must.

"Here, in this universe, the outward trappings were less picturesque, I suppose. A man in a boat, escaping to help the Allies. But his escape was necessary. In the light of what happened since, you can maybe guess why. So Holger Danske arose to see that he did get free. I was . . . weeks? . . . gone in that Carolingian world, and returned to the same minute on this. Time is a funny thing."

"What became of you afterward?" I inquired.

He chuckled. "I had a devil of a time explaining why and how I'd peeled to the buff before charging the enemy. But we were in a hurry, and went our separate ways before the strain on my wits got too great. Since then I've been plain Holger Carlsen. What else could I do?" He shrugged. "When I came to the knowledge of myself as the Defender, I broke the hosts of Chaos in that world. Then, because of the spell, I was drawn back to finish my task on this side. Once the crisis was past in both worlds, the job done . . . well, equilibrium had been re-established. There was no unbalanced force to send me across space-time. So I stayed."

He looked wearily at me. "Of course, I know what you're thinking," he said. "Delusions and so on. I don't blame you. But thanks for the use of your ear."

"I'm not quite sure what to think," I answered. "Tell me, though, why are you hunting books?"

"Old books," he said. "*Grimoires*. Treatises on magic. Morgan sent me here once." His fist crashed on the table. "And I'll find the way back for myself!"

I haven't seen or heard from him for years. No one has. Well, people do disappear. Perhaps he disappeared to the place he spoke of—always assuming the story true, a matter in which I suspend judgment. I hope he did.

But meanwhile new storms are rising. It may be that we shall need Holger Danske again.